Alki Zei

' Zei is an award-winning Greek author of over a
en books for children including: *Wildcat under Glass,*
r's War, The Purple Umbrella, Alice In Marble Land
The Sound of the Dragon's Feet.

992, she won the National Award for Children's
ature (Greece) and has been nominated for the
s Christian Andersen Award and the Astrid
gren Memorial Award for Literature. Her books
been translated into many languages.

s Web has been awarded *The Ibby Prize for Best*
for Teenagers (Greece) and the *Bookworms Prize for*
Readers (France).

John Thornley, translator

Thornley researched 20th century Greek music in
ens with a British Council scholarship, conducted
ra in Germany and Italy, and was a senior producer
BBC Radio 3. His play *The Death of Anton Webern* was
inated for the Italia Prize, and his World Music
io series won the Brno Prize and two Sony awards.
has made literary translations from Greek, French,
lian, Latin, German and Norwegian, including
p etry by Elytis, Éluard, Mörike and Celan, and *Sabina,*
a play about the psychoanalyst Sabina Spielrein. He is
currently writing a biography of Greek composer Nikos
Skalkottas.

We gratefully acknowledge financial assistance from The Arts Council of England.
First published in the UK in 2007 by Aurora Metro Publications Ltd.
info@aurorametro.com www.aurorametro.com
020 8898 4488 smallpublisher.blogspot.com

Published in agreement with Bookboom, Book Marketing and Promotion Services, 37 Roudou St., GR151 22, Athens, Greece.

Translation copyright © 2007 John Thornley
Cover Design : Joe Webb www.etchdesign.co.uk
Photographs: Copyright © 2007 Nuno Silva/Agency istockphoto.com
Production: Gillian Wakeling

With thanks to: The Hellenic Centre, Angelica Vouloumoulou, The National Book Centre, Athens, Judy Heckstall-Smith, Clare Chatham, Aidan Jenkins, Sharanjit Jasser.

ISBN 978 0-9551566-1-8

Printed by Ashford Colour Press, UK.

ALKI ZEI

TINA'S WEB

translated by

John Thornley

AURORA METRO PRESS

Reviews of Alki Zei's work:

'Written with a fine and original humour, with a discreet sense of the innocent happiness of childhood that becomes even more touching within the borders of a world that collapses... the themes of the novel are universal.'

New York Times

'A book that one reads without a pause, written in an amusing style with humour and spirit.'

The Observer

'The most interesting novel for children and young people of the year.'

Le Monde

'Astonishing, expressive, amusing, compassionate, one of the big hits of this year.'

Le Nouvel Observateur

'Alki Zei uses a narrative technique of understated tones. The dramatic story she tells is not directly revealed but is made clear for the reader by suggestion: the image of the wounded owl describes in a masterly way the emptiness covered with spiders' webs, in which her heroes struggle to find something to hold on to. They are victims and perpetrators at the same time and, while trying to save and be saved, they drag themselves and others to destruction.'

Katherimerini Newspaper

'The works of Alki Zei have a special quality: they break down the boundaries between reading for children and adolescents, and reading for adults – she is read by everyone.'

To Vima newspaper

To Anna

'...for the children who were lost
to the dragon's well
to the old hag's cave.'

from the song *The Lost Children*
by Dionysis Savvopoulos

CHAPTER ONE

They say it's not possible to remember the moment you were born. That the first images of your life come into your mind much later, and even those are fragmented and cloudy. Well, that's what they say.

Soon I'll be thirteen. But I can still see the moment I was born, very clearly, right in front of me. They think because I've heard them talking about it, I've started to imagine . . . But it's not imagining at all. I can actually see it, like the slides from our holiday in Denmark that dad brings out to show his friends. How could I have just dreamt it up? I can't imagine anything. At school, even the Greek language teacher – Greek Geek, the kids call her – she's always telling me: 'You have no imagination.'

Stuff that happens I can describe – very well, actually. That's why I'm inconsistent. Sometimes I get nineteen out of twenty for an essay, sometimes only eleven. I mean, everything about me's uneven. I'm either up, or down. I can love, I can hate. But however hard they try to convince me I can't remember the moment I came out of mum's tummy, I absolutely know I can.

I didn't yell, unlike that baby I saw being born in a TV documentary. I was wrapped in cobwebs. I was fighting with my hands and feet to free myself. Someone said – it can't have been dad, he couldn't even face going into the birth unit – perhaps it was the doctor, because it was a man's voice: 'I've never seen a new-born child covered in cobwebs before.' And then they say I can't possibly remember it!

Whenever I gave a push to get out, I got even more tangled up. Finally the doctor cut the threads with a pair of scissors, set me free, caught me by the feet and lifted me high up. But I'd got so exhausted, I couldn't manage a peep. Of course, I can't recall every detail, like how I got into my cradle with my gran bending over me. But I heard very clearly what gran said to the nurse: 'It's yellow, just like a little corpse.' 'Don't say that, madam, that's a terrible thing to say.'

Truth is, my gran never stops telling people how I came into the world shrouded in cobwebs, how I never made a sound, and how I looked like a little corpse. But it's not just that I've heard it from her. I can actually remember it. Even now when I'm asleep I often see myself entangled in a net, and I have to kick out to free myself. I only weighed five pounds five ounces. Of course, I can't remember that. My mum wrote it down in a book called *Our Child's First Years*. It's full of questions, and mum answered them all. Where I was born, the date, day of the week, time of day, how much I weighed . . . There's nothing about the webs though, because there's no question that goes: 'Was your child born wrapped in a spider's web?' But there ought to be.

Well, according to the book, I was slow at doing everything. Slow at turning my head, at sitting up, standing up, crawling around, walking, even slow at starting to speak. But it's not true that I didn't say my first words until I was two. I'm sure I was speaking a lot earlier than that, but saying the words inside myself. When gran asked me why I wasn't eating my cream pudding, I used to reply silently: 'Just because!'

I used to talk to the cats in the yard, to the fish in the bowl, most of all to the ladybirds that flew onto my fingers. They weren't afraid of me, and I wasn't afraid of them.

When they left me at gran's house, I'd sit down on a little stool, and I wouldn't budge until they came to fetch me. 'You should take her to the doctor,' gran would tell Mum. 'That child doesn't speak, not a squeak out of her. She just sits there like a flowerpot.' And maybe she was thinking to herself: 'Like a little corpse.' Mum insisted, that at home, I was always jumping around on the sofas and doing the voices of dogs, cats, even donkeys – though I'd never actually seen one. Gran would shake her head in disbelief.

My gran's called Ismeni, and dad wanted to name me after her. But she wouldn't hear of it. She was convinced I was going to die, and she didn't want to waste her name on me. They christened me Konstantina, and I survived. I never knew my grandad, but he was called Konstantinos.

Gran didn't like me, and I didn't like her. There was only one child she really loved; my cousin

Venetia. She was the daughter of Auntie Maria, my dad's sister. I say 'she was', because Venetia's not alive any more. She died two years before I was born. Or rather, she burnt to death. They'd bought her a little nylon skirt for Easter. She put it on and ran to show it off to her godmother, who lived a couple of houses away. The godmother went into the kitchen to get her some orange juice and Venetia found a box of matches and went out to the balcony to light the candles they'd stuck on the parapet railing for the Good Friday procession that was passing by in the street below.

She was ten years old, was Venetia, and she was utterly charming and totally pretty, blah blah blah. Just like the famous city of Venice, according to gran, though she's never been there in her life. In gran's house, in the lounge, in her bedroom – everywhere in fact – there are photos of Venetia as a baby, Venetia as a little girl, Venetia as a ballerina, Venetia dressed as Marie Antoinette, as Snow White, as a water-sprite, and as a Venetian lady – in a carnival costume her godmother had brought her back from Venice. She had blonde hair, waves and waves of it falling down to her waist, and chubby rosy cheeks. But her eyes were dull, a sort of watery blue-grey, even if gran says they're 'expressive'. In all the photos, they gaze out into the distance, looking nowhere in particular.

Perhaps that's why I never liked going to gran's. She really got on my nerves with dear little Venetia. Good thing she died. Since I hated her dead, just imagine how much I'd hate her if she was still alive.

Gran didn't come to see us much. 'Well, since you've gone to live at the end of the earth . . . ' she used to say to dad, every time they grumbled about it.

She lives in the Kypseli area, not that far from the centre of Athens, while ever since I was born we'd rented a place out in Argiroupolis, down towards the airport. But I don't think it was the distance that stopped her. It was because I was living there, the little corpse, scarcely five and a half measly pounds, who only opened her mouth once in a blue moon – since I was saying everything silently to myself – and Venetia was gone. Venetia who could talk, sing, recite poems, and who didn't slouch like me, but stood up straight, as straight as a wax taper at a christening.

Whenever they asked gran to come and stay with me, because I was sick a lot of the time, sometimes with tonsilitis, sometimes diarrhoea, but mostly with bronchitis – as soon as she came into the house I'd hear her saying: 'So that child is ill again!' Before going to work, mum would show her the medicines I had to take, and leave books and board games on a little bookshelf close to my bed.

But gran wouldn't read to me, or play with me. She sat in a chair next to me and read her newspaper just like a kid swotting for exams. If I was burning with a fever or choked with coughing, she'd stop reading for a bit to give me a spoonful of syrup, then she'd immerse herself again in her paper. Each time she turned a page it gave me a shock, like hearing a gust of wind catching an open window and slamming it to. 'Gran, stop turning the pages,' I said in my drowsy stupor, and I could hear the pages of the newspaper going 'dung-phwum!', banging to and fro as if on some deserted house covered with cobwebs.

When mum and dad told her we were going to Germany, because they'd been appointed to teach in the Greek sections they have in some German schools – mum and dad are both teachers – I think gran was glad to get rid of me, not to have to keep on putting up with me being ill, having to ask me something three times before getting an answer, or wondering why I had hair as straight as a ruler, when all my family on both sides have curly hair, or wondering why I was so thin, why I had a slouch, why I was so pale – 'like a little corpse' – and why my eyes had such a searching look. I've no idea what kind of look I had, but I know I certainly wasn't gazing out into the distance with dreamy blue eyes – mine are a dark chestnut, almost black, and they took up a lot of room on my tiny blob of a face.

So gran was really pleased, I'm sure of that, but she still argued with dad about our going to live in Germany. 'You've forgotten all about your father, apparently.' She hated the Germans, because during the Second World War, 'when they invaded Greece and enslaved our poor country', they caught Grandad and put him in prison – though he managed to escape. But she couldn't stand the British either, because something else happened in Greece after the War had ended, and this time it was the British who arrested grandad and interned him somewhere in Africa. As for the Americans, she didn't like them one bit, because she said all the evils of our country and the whole world were caused by them, and she got really mad when I put my rock music on full blast. The only ones she liked were the Russians, not the ones they have now, but the previous ones, the Soviets, as she called them. 'Going to live with the Germans? The very idea!' She just couldn't stomach it at all. Dad laughed and teased her, telling her that it was time to take the needle off the record. I didn't understand what he meant, but I didn't care anyway, and I was pleased we were leaving.

I'd never travelled before, except on the bus, on summer trips with gran to Karpenissi, up in the Roumeli mountains. But now I'd be boarding a plane, and we'd be going to 'a really lovely city called Aachen'. You have to pronounce the 'a' twice, it's like taking a deep breath. Dad had already been there, and he'd rented a flat for us. I'd be taking German language lessons in Athens in the summer, and when we went to live in Aachen they'd send me to the German school, to the proper first year class, except that for some of the lessons, while the other children had painting or craftwork or something similar, I'd be doing German on my own. In the afternoon I'd be attending the Greek school, an independent department of the German school. Dad explained all the details to me, and he said it was better not to mention it to gran, because 'she'll just get angry and make a lot of fuss'.

I think they'd concealed something else from her: the whole of last year, he and mum had been going to a German language institute in Athens and they'd been studying until late at night, when I was asleep.

When the time came for us to say goodbye, gran gave me a yellow woollen bonnet that she'd knitted herself, 'because it's very cold where you're going'. She'd never knitted me anything, apart from a little jacket when I was a baby. I'd never have thought she could knit, if I hadn't seen Venetia wearing knitwear of all different colours and patterns in the photos. There was one thing of hers I was actually very envious of. It was a red pullover, with a row of blue deer on the front.

A yellow bonnet! I never wore it.

Mum couldn't keep it to herself, she said: 'Anything but yellow, please. It doesn't suit her at all.' Gran replied that she couldn't knit with a colour she hadn't already used, and the yellow was all she had left. 'A little corpse with a yellow bonnet', I said to myself. I don't know what she said to herself, she just came and kissed me on the top of my head. I tried to hug her, but my hands stayed woodenly at my side, and I just said: 'Bye, gran'.

At that moment, none of us could imagine that a day would come when she and I would live together in her house in Kypseli, and that this was the last time I'd call her 'gran'. Later, I'd give her another name that would stick forever.

I'm caught up in the cobwebs and struggling to free myself. Slowly, I open my eyes. I've got mixed up with the bedclothes. I never used to get tangled up with my feather duvet. I sit up in bed, with the sheet twisted round my neck. The heavy grey blankets are prickling my legs.

– Your milk.

An unfamiliar voice. Not mum's, not dad's.

Opposite I can see the narrow window. Horrible blue curtains with red roses, ughhh.

I'm at my gran's house. Waking up is always the same, even after six months. I think, it must be a nightmare, and when I wake up, I'll be underneath my good old feather duvet.

– Your milk.

It's the third time she's called out. So I have to reply:

– OK, Farmor.

That's what Sigrid called her grandmother. Sigrid was my schoolmate and bestest friend in Aachen. She's Swedish, and the Swedish word for gran is 'Farmor'. That's the gran on the father's side, on the mother's she's called 'Mormor'. 'Farmor' really suited my gran: Mormor sounds far too sweet.

It's Sunday, I'm sure of that. So why am I being woken up at the crack of dawn? I look at my watch. OK then, nine o'clock. At this time, in Aachen, my dad would go out and get us warm bread rolls. I could smell them while I was still half asleep. Now Brigitte will be eating them . . . How suddenly everything can fall apart. 'But didn't you notice anything?' gran keeps on at me. But even if I wanted to answer her the first time, I couldn't manage it. 'No, Farmor, not a thing.'

CHAPTER TWO

They say when you're drowning at sea, before you go under for the last time, you see your whole life pass before you, like a film in the cinema. Well, now that I'm drowning on dry land, I can see my whole life in Aachen flashing past.

Our house, on a wide road lined with trees, and with flowerbeds in the middle.

We used to live on the third floor, and on the ground floor was the bakery that sold the bread rolls. My room was large, with a big bed, almost a double, made of brass, like in the olden days. Above it was a hoop, and a canopy like a mosquito net covering it over completely, perfect for snuggling down and daydreaming. I'd seen it in a shop window, when I went with mum and dad to buy furniture. 'That's the one I want.' They laughed. 'Let's treat her,' said Dad, and they bought it for me. After they delivered it, I used to lie on it for hours. Sometimes I'd just hide away under the netting, sometimes I'd open it and look through the big window that took up the whole of one wall, and opposite I'd see the lights of the Annastrasse – a quiet street with lovely old houses, decked out with antique street lamps.

That's where I'd go with my dad for a walk after my lessons, even when it had started to get dark. When it snowed, the snowflakes sparkled in the lamplight. On Fridays, when neither of us had school the following day, dad and I would stroll all around the pedestrian zone. We'd do some window shopping – or rather, I would – and we'd end up in a large café, the *King's College*, where they had chairs made of yellow cane, and wooden tables. I'd have a hot chocolate and dad would drink a beer. If we were late getting back, mum would laugh and say 'Have you two been throwing our money around again?'

It was on that street with the lamps that I used to tell dad all my secrets. 'So, Tina, my teeny', dad would say, 'what news today?' And I'd start talking and never stop, mostly about school, which I adored.

I loved my school the moment I saw it. Although before we went in on the first day, my heart was pounding like mad, and my hands, held by mum on one side and dad on the other, were sweating buckets.

We came into a large courtyard paved with green-grey stone slabs and a big over-hanging roof all around the sides.

'Herr Heiner, the headmaster, is expecting us in his office,' says mum. We passed along a corridor with beige and cherry-red floor tiles. The corridor seemed endless, but along its whole length there were windows, and on the ledges there were flower pots, each one with different flowers and plants.

There were paintings all along the wall on the other side. My heart seemed to stop beating altogether – I was lost in a daze.

We climbed a staircase; instead of banisters, it had a white metallic mesh with a red rail on top. We reached the first floor and stood in front of a door that dad said was the head teacher's office. I probably went pale. I expect I looked like a little corpse. Mum knocked on the door and dad turned round and smiled at me. 'Be a brave girl, Tina – as we said, he's the best.'

The door opened automatically, and dad practically dragged me through the doorway, but before we'd got properly inside, a man came up and stood there before us. He wasn't very tall, and he had reddish hair and blue eyes; he was smiling, revealing a set of snow-white teeth.

My heart stopped beating like a drum. He made a bow, gave me a kiss on the cheek and said in Greek: 'Welcome, my dear child.' Dad had told me that Herr Heiner was passionate about Greece and was learning Greek. He went to his desk, a large one, piled high with papers, in the middle of which you could just see a blue vase of yellow roses.

He told us to sit down, and I sat right on the edge of a chair. If I'd moved at all, I'd have fallen off.

Farmor, if only you could have heard what he said to me. How he could see from my face that I would get on just fine, and that I looked 'intelligent and determined'. Then he got up and held my hand to take me to my class.

Mum and dad looked at me as if to say 'Be a brave girl!' but I didn't need any encouragement. I walked through the corridors at the headmaster's side, and tried not to slouch, and looked all around with my 'intelligent and determined' look, until we reached the classroom.

While Herr Heiner was talking with the teacher, I glanced round the room, with its large windows. Here too there were pot plants on the ledges and paintings on the walls. Each of the children was sitting at their own individual desk.

Almost all of them had flaxen blond hair, with blue eyes, but I could pick out one with slanting dark eyes, and a black boy with curly hair. All of them were staring straight at me.

Herr Heiner patted my head and left the classroom. The teacher, a blonde young woman with a freckled face, showed me to an empty desk in the front row, where I sat down. At the desk next to mine, there was a girl with flaming-red hair, who gave me a smile.

The teacher went and wrote on a massive board, that took up the whole wall. It's lucky that I did German lessons in the summer before we left Greece, so at least I could recognise the letters.

Then Frau Stephani – I realised that was the teacher's name, because she pointed to herself and said 'Frau Stephani' – said out loud, one by one, the words she'd written on the board, and I watched her mouth, to see how to pronounce them.

In the afternoon school, the Greek one, I had no

difficulties. Mum and dad had already taught me how to read in Greek. Here the first and second Greek primary school classes did their lessons together – there were eleven of us kids in all.

Luckily, I don't have mum as my teacher. That would be weird. She teaches the fifth and sixth years, and the kids love her. As soon as they see her, they run and throw their arms around her, chanting 'Mrs Stel-la, Mrs Stel-la!' I'm really proud of my mum.

One day, we met Herr Heiner in the corridor. He started off talking to her in German, but then with a twinkle in his eye, he said in Greek: 'Mrs Stella, you are the diamond of our school.'

I wish Farmor could hear that. I know she doesn't like mum much; at least she didn't in the first few years after she'd married dad. If dad hadn't been so persistent, maybe she wouldn't even be my mum!

When mum was little, poor thing, her parents were moving around from town to town, and she had to change school five times. Small towns, some of them, where they didn't even have electricity. Her dad was a police officer, and he had to go wherever they sent him.

During the Civil War – when was that, Farmor? OK, I remember now, after the Germans left in 1944. I'm always getting the dates mixed up, what with all those wars and battles I hear you constantly talking about with your friends. Anyway, as I was saying, in the Civil War they arrested my grandad Konstantinos again, and exiled him to a camp on one of the islands.

On the boat they sent him on, along with the other communist prisoners, there was a police officer keeping guard. He was my other grandfather, my mum's dad!

Farmor maintains that if they trusted him to guard such a famous rebel as my grandad, he must have been an out-and-out fascist. Mind you, even when she's telling you the story of Little Red Riding Hood, she'd claim the real reason the wolf gobbled the kid up was that he was a fascist.

Back then dad hadn't met mum yet, and by the time he had, both my grandads had died.

When dad told her he was going to marry mum, Farmor kicked up an enormous fuss: 'Your father will be turning in his grave.'

She used to say that a lot, though I can't see how poor old grandad could turn in his grave. But dad's stubborn when he gets an idea into his head, Farmor's the same – so am I, actually. So dad did marry mum after all – and by then she didn't have a soul in the world, as her mother had died too.

I'd be really fed up if dad had listened to Farmor; it'd mean I'd have a different mum now, not my own mum,who's really great and the 'diamond of the school,' as Herr Heiner says. I'm afraid I'm not the 'diamond of the class', though at the end of the school year, I did manage to come third.

The German school is no bed of roses. There are four years in primary school, and if you're not very bright, you don't go on to the grammar school, where there are another eight years before you can get into university. Instead you have to do six years in a normal secondary school, and then you can do courses at professional or technical schools. Mum says that's very unfair, because a child shouldn't be judged at the age of ten for the rest of their life.

Apart from Sigrid, the girl with the red hair, who became my best mate, I made friends with lots of children in my class. Among the boys, my favourite was the black kid, Diagoras. Strange, he has a Greek name, but dad explained that in some parts of Africa they have a custom of taking names from Ancient Greece. Diagoras is top of the class, and however hard David tries – he's second – he can't catch up with him, particularly in arithmetic, where Diagoras can subtract thirteen from forty-nine in his head, just like that, while the rest of us can just about do three plus one.

Shortly after Sigrid and I first got to know each other, she gave me a present; a diary with a lock, and a little key that I always have hanging round my neck. On the cover there's a bright red cat. 'Like me', she said as she handed it over. Its eyes are really beady, a deep blue, like hers.

Good thing I have it. Now I'm stuck at Farmor's house, I'm reading and re-reading it after shutting myself in my tiny room.

When I first arrived, Farmor put a little bed in her room so we could both sleep there. We had a row about that, and finally her friends, the three Demetrias – actually only one of them is called Demetria, like the earth mother goddess, but that's what Farmor calls them all – they persuaded her to give me a little room that she was using as a storeroom. And they helped her to empty it and move heaps of cardboard boxes, shoving some of them under the bed, and others on top of the cupboard.

– What are you keeping all this for? asked one of the earth mothers, shifting the tenth box.

– Why do you need to know? answered Farmor, before adding: Since you were the ones encouraging her, you can help do the lifting.

By evening, my room was ready.

One of the Demetrias rushed out and bought a cupboard with a plastic zip-up door, so I could keep my clothes straight, and as a desk they put in a little orange formica table.

Farmor unearthed these dreadful curtains, the blue ones with the red roses, the second Demi persuaded her to iron them, and the third Demi bought me a little imitation dog, just like a real one – the only really new thing I had in the room.

Instead of saying 'thanks' I threw them a look of contempt and said:

– OK, I'll go into my cage.

Before I closed the door, I heard Farmor saying:

– I told you how ill-bred she is! Don't make excuses for her.

I don't know what 'ill-bred' means, but I can't imagine it's anything good. Yet it's not the Demetrias' fault, and I shouldn't behave like that towards them. After all they half-killed themselves to fix up the room for me.

So I'm shutting myself in my cage, I'm sitting at my little orange formica desk, and I'm staring at my books and notebooks, without looking at them. I've pulled the curtains, because the window looks onto the light well of the building.

'To the bestest friend I'll ever have.' Sigrid's handwriting, in German, on the first page of my diary.

So how will she cope, now she doesn't have me sitting next to her in class? Will she find another best friend? And we had so many dreams for the years to come . . .

I open a page at random.

Friday

When I came home with dad from our walk, I found Sigrid waiting for me at home. She had a very knowing, secretive look. 'Go to your room', she said, 'you'll find something in there.'

I ran, and straight away I saw what the something was. A little hamster, eating a leaf of lettuce in the middle of its cage and watching me with its beady eyes. She'd got it for me as a present.

We decided to call it Leonardo di Caprio, after the star of Titanic. I'm mad about him.

I'm mad about the hamster too.

Saturday

Today Sigrid slept at our place. There's plenty of room for both of us in my bed.

Tomorrow we don't have school, so we can have a proper gossip before we fall asleep. Sigrid's parents are divorced. She lives with her mum, and on Saturdays she goes to her dad's. Her dad has married again and his wife is going to have a baby.

Sigrid is really glad she's going to get a brother, even if it's only a half-brother.

I can't really imagine what it's like not to live with your mum and dad, and only see one of them every Saturday.

Sunday

This morning we went ice-skating with dad. Mum went to Mr Michalis's place so they can study together, as they're both taking a course in German literature at the university.

In any case, mum isn't one for the ice-rink. She takes me to concerts, to the theatre, and to the Roncalli Circus from Vienna – they visit Aachen twice a year.

I go absolutely wild when I'm rushing around on ice. But how could I possibly get up to Sigrid's level – she's got ice in her blood. In Sweden, she probably learned to skate before she learned to walk. She skates so beautifully, and she can do all kinds of fancy moves.

How I'd love to be an ice dancer!

I don't miss a single ice-skating programme on television. Afterwards I usually snuggle into bed, underneath the netting, and I imagine that the white canopy is a drift of snow on which I'm doing the most daring routines. I haven't told anyone I want to be an ice dancer. Not even Sigrid. I'd feel stupid talking about it – I don't know any queen of the ice-skating world who has a stoop and who's as pale as a little corpse. Never mind that most Sundays I can't exercise because my bronchial attacks choose the worst moment to come along. They've taken me to heaps of doctors, and the only thing that does any good at all is a syrup dad gets on private prescription. And I do exercises for my back, but I can't imagine it getting any better, so my whole life I'll be like this.

And something else I'd really like to do – that's horse riding. I'm crazy about horses, and in my room I've a gigantic poster of a beautiful beautiful horse. But how can I even go there? Have you ever seen a horse rider with a hunched back? I once saw a king on a film on television, he was galloping on a horse that was almost collapsing under his massive hunchback. It was late and they didn't let me see how it ended. But then he was a king, he could have ridden back to front if he'd wanted to.

Now and then I go with Brigitte, who's a schoolmate, and her mum, Frau Sabrina – she's a teacher at the school where dad also teaches – to watch Brigitte horse riding. She lets me pat her horse and give him a lump of sugar.

Once Brigitte helped me mount, and we went for a proper ride together. She says I did pretty well and I should get my own horse. She'd ride alongside me to help me, and after one or two goes I'd be able to ride on my own. But I know she's only saying all that because she really wants to be my best friend.

Out. Of. The. Question.

She reminds me of Venetia. She has the same fair hair, reaching down to her waist, and above all dreamy eyes that look into the distance; and then the way she sits bolt upright on her horse. Funniest of all, dad has now got it into his head that he should take up horse riding as well. When he was a boy, he says, he used to go riding in Karpenissi – only mules, of course, not horses, but there can't be a big difference because he did really well at the first try. Brigitte and Frau Sabrina cheered him on wildly.

In my dreams, I often see myself galloping on a horse, sitting up as straight as a die, but however fast I ride, my back curves over and I end up like that king in the film. So it's goodbye to that as well.

Never mind that I'm tone-deaf, I sing flat and they won't let me sing in the school choir, and I can't draw either – so I don't have any talent at all.

Dad tries to console me by saying that I'm sharp as a razor at arithmetic. But what use is arithmetic to an ice-dancer or a horse rider?

Wednesday – The Wolf With a Hole instead of a Soul

Poor old wolf! They really made a fool of him. Today our teacher took us to see the Cathedral. Just outside it there's the statue of a wolf, and right in the middle of the wolf's tummy there's a big hole.

Our teacher told us that in olden times, during the reign of Charlemagne, the inhabitants of the city of Aachen wanted to build a church. But the wars had emptied all the coffers. They got together to see what they could do, and then one of the people stood up and said he'd give them all the money they needed, but on condition that once the church was finished, he would take the soul of whoever was the first to go inside. The others took a good look at him, and noticed that his feet were like the hooves of a goat. They realised he was the Devil, but they really wanted a church so they accepted his terms. They gathered together again when the church was finished – the Cathedral as it is today – to try to find a way to rid themselves of the Devil, and then a shepherd suggested they should catch the wolf that came down every day to steal his flock of sheep, and put him in a cage, then let him loose inside the church.

The Devil had said he'd take the soul of the first one to enter the church. But he hadn't made it clear whether it would have to be a human being or if it could be an animal. So they caught the wolf and did what the shepherd told them.

The Devil went into the church, rushed up to the wolf, stuck his hand inside him and took away his soul.

Afterwards he realised his mistake, but a promise is a promise, and the Devil keeps his word like a gentleman.

And so they put up the statue of the wolf at the entrance to the Cathedral, because one way or another they owed him a favour.

That's how I feel now. As if they'd made a hole and taken my soul out. I flick quickly through the diary, and I come across the pages where I've written only a few words on each page.

I couldn't find the courage to write any more. But I can remember it all by heart.

6th May

Annastrasse – The End

That's all I've written right at the top of the page, nothing else. Just that. For the day when my whole life changed forever. *'But didn't you notice anything at all?' 'No, Farmor, nothing.'*

Dad took me for a walk on the Annastrasse. Mum stopped us at the door on our way out, and gave me a thicker jacket, because it was quite chilly and she was worried about my bronchitis. In May, the days are already very long in Aachen. It's light until ten o'clock at night . . .

Today, although it wasn't yet six, the streetlights were already on, because there was such a fog that you couldn't see beyond your nose. I like the Annastrasse wrapped in mist, its lamps shine out like lighthouses in the middle of the ocean.

Dad held my hand, squeezing it hard. 'That hurts.' 'Tina, . . . I . . . I've . . . I need to tell you something.'

What's wrong with dad? Whenever he has something to tell me he comes right out with it, even when he knows it'll start a row. Now he was standing still and looking me right in the eye. He took my hand, then let it go. 'Go on dad, tell me.'

We were standing underneath a streetlamp. 'Would you like to go to *King's College* for your hot chocolate?' 'Tell me, dad.'

I was afraid he was going to tell me we were going back to Greece for ever. He knew how scared I was that might happen. Obviously that was what was holding him back. 'Tina . . . '

And then he began to spell it out, and at the start I couldn't for the life of me understand what he was trying to say, but as he went on, I felt my legs shaking, as if they were about to give way.

So he started telling me how much he and mum loved each other, and what a marvellous woman my mother is, being so good at everything, going to university to get a German language diploma – did he think I didn't know? – but that sometimes a time comes when even if people love one another, they realise they can't live together any more, and perhaps, if they decide to live apart . . . 'Tina – don't shake like that.'

It wasn't just me shaking, so were the lights and the whole of the Annastrasse, then dad started shaking too, and he suggested that we should go and drink a hot chocolate, and I shouted: 'Let's go home, I want to go home, to mum.' Dad said mum had gone to do some studying with Mr Michalis, and I tried to pull him towards our house, while he was trying to pull me in the direction of *King's College*. A policeman came up, looked suspiciously at dad, and asked 'What's wrong with the little girl?'

I was afraid he'd arrest dad, because recently there had been some cases of weirdos accosting girls, and at school they'd warned us to be careful. 'We're playing a game to see which of us can pull the hardest', said dad, and the policeman smiled and went off.

At home, before dad could put the key in the door, mum opened it for us. 'You didn't go to study with Michalis?' asked dad. Mum shook her head and gave me a hug, and we all three went and sat on the large sofa in the living-room, hugging each other and crying. How lovely that was!

But then, the next few days – as I remember it, they weren't lovely at all. In the evenings sometimes it was dad looking after me, and sometimes it was mum. Whichever one was out came home once I'd gone to sleep. Whenever dad suggested we go for our walk on the Annastrasse, I ignored him completely.

Saturday

Washed-out Weekends

At the weekends, we don't get friends coming round any more; no more of those endless discussions about whether there should be independent Greek schools for the Greeks in Germany, or whether people should send their kids to the German schools – like me – and do Greek classes in the evening. They all used to shout and argue, but it was fun, because after all the arguments they'd eat and drink and begin to sing Greek songs, with dad to the fore – he has a really lovely voice. Shame he didn't pass it on to me!

Mr Michalis used to come round a lot, the one who goes to university with mum. He talks more than any of them, and if Farmor could hear him she'd be over the moon. He doesn't like Germany, and he can't wait for his two years to pass so he can get back to Greece, 'even if the education system there does have loads of problems'.

Luckily mum and dad don't have to go back home, even when their five years are up. They've made the big decision to stay in Germany at least until I leave school and mum's university course is finished. They resigned from their Greek state school jobs and now they're being paid just by the German government. Farmor knows nothing about it: she's always asking them: 'OK, fine, but why aren't you coming back?'

'We got an extension', answers dad, without going into it.

I didn't want to go back to Greece at all. Whatever Mr Michalis says, I really like Aachen. It may not have the sun or the Acropolis. But it's got parks, neat buildings, fountains, spotlessly clean roads, warm bread rolls and apple strudel with cream, as well as my lovely bronze horses in front of the station, that seem so lifelike, as if they're just about to break into a gallop. I go over and stroke them whenever I'm passing.

There are four of them, and I've given them names: Hasty, Haughty, Speedy, and Softy – he's the one who leans his head gently to the side. I'm sure I'd be able to ride him.

Saturday

Silence at Home. Final Verdict – No Appeal.

From then on, at the weekends it was completely silent at home. Either dad wasn't there, or mum, and I didn't feel like doing anything. I just coughed and coughed. I couldn't have gone to the ice rink like that, even if I'd wanted to.

Sigrid came to see me, and I asked her: 'What's it like when your parents split up?'

She couldn't remember what it was like when they were living together, because she was only three when her parents separated, but now she thinks it's great. She has two homes, two really nice bedrooms, she celebrates her birthday twice, and in the summer she goes for a month's holiday with her mum, then has another month somewhere else with her dad. On top of that she has as many as four grannies and three grandads. Two grannies and one grandad from her own family in Sweden. Then another gran and grandad from her dad's wife, who live in Aachen. And the others left over are from her mum's husband; they live in Denmark, because her mum's husband is Danish. Sigrid likes the Danish ones best, and at Christmas she'll be going to spend it with them in Copenhagen. It may be like that for Sigrid, but I'm not three years old, and I've only got one gran – Farmor.

I couldn't stop coughing, and the doctor said 'it's not a psychological problem, not at all', and that since we have such a beautiful country with so much sun, I should go there for a short time to shake off the bronchitis.

For several days I didn't go to school, just sat in bed under my net. My fever had finished, but not the coughing.

In the mornings, I did Greek lessons with mum, and then in the afternoon, Brigitte's mum came, Frau Sabrina – tall and extremely pretty – so I could do German. I like her a lot more than her daughter, or rather I used to like her, before I found out that she's going to be my second mum. I was reminded, don't know why, of a little poem one of gran's friends taught us when I was very little: *'Now she'll have two ma-mas, both of us will feed her soup and put on her pyja-mas'.*

A second mum's all very well, but Brigitte as a sister – never! Up till now she hasn't managed even to be my friend, let alone my sister! I told dad straight out. 'But it's the final verdict, with no appeal,' he murmured.

It was the first time I'd heard that expression, and I didn't ask what it meant. When I did find out, I realised suddenly that everything was a 'final verdict with no appeal'.

And Mr Michalis will be my dad number two! Luckily he'd got no kids, otherwise I'd be up to my ears in brothers and sisters.

But when I came to live with Farmor I found out the whole truth – that Mr Michalis and mum were going to have a little boy and he'd be my new little brother. *'But didn't you notice anything?' 'No, Farmor, nothing at all.'*

The whole world is upside down, and I'm just sitting here coughing and taking my medicine . . .

At any rate, after my lessons at home, somehow or other I managed to finish the year at my German school, and got a certificate for completing the Greek one too.

Thursday

Since they love me, since they love one another, then WHY????

Mum and dad had never shown me more love than they did now. And I'd never seen them be so affectionate to one another. That made me think it was all just a big game, like the one where you stand behind a row of chairs, the music plays, and when it stops you run to sit down in somebody else's place. So in dad's chair sits Mr Michalis, and in mum's, Frau Sabrina.

But it isn't a game, it's a 'final verdict with no appeal'. And what about me? Where am I going to live? It could even be with Farmor!

They didn't come right out with it, because they couldn't agree. The doctor suggested I should have a change of climate, then one child psychologist advised that I go to stay with Farmor, while the other – because they'd asked two to examine me – said I should remain in Aachen so as not to be moved from my home. The first insisted 'for the good of the child, you should separate from her for a little while, for her to get some perspective, and to be some way off when the changes occur'. Sometimes I'd hear odd phrases, then hear them all over again when they actually said them to me adding: 'It's for your own good, Tina'.

For my own good? My own good is to stay with my mum and dad, and for them to stay together.

Even lovely Herr Heiner agreed that I should leave. He wasn't my head teacher any more, but since I'd started going to grammar school he'd become one of the closest friends our family had, and we saw a lot of him. The truth is that both mum and dad were finding it difficult to make the decision.

As strange as it sounds, I was the one who decided, in the end.

Since it hurts them so much to be apart from me, let's stay together.

Imagine if I'd told them, I don't want to be your child any more, I want another mum and another dad. What would they have made of that, then? I'm wondering, is this what happens with almost everybody? Parents live together for a bit and then split up? Because now I think about it, in my class of twenty-two children, at least fifteen have divorced parents. But it never occurred to me that something like that could happen. *'You didn't notice anything?' 'No, Farmor, not a thing.'*

The doctor, the child psychologist, Herr Heiner, mum, dad – they're all trying to make me understand.

Monday, Tuesday, Wednesday, and Other Days

The doctor promised me that if I live in Greece for a year, I'll get rid of my cough and the bronchitis. I didn't think it was all that important. But Herr Heiner had a way of talking you into things. When he wanted to discuss it with me, he didn't ask me to go and see him at his school; instead he came and picked me up in his car and took me to *Café Roncalli*, which had just newly opened (it was named after the Viennese circus) and I'd not been yet.

As soon as we got inside the door, I forgot all my worries. There was a great marble staircase leading to the floor above, where there were balconies all around, like boxes in the theatre. The staircase was carved and gilded, and halfway up, on a landing, a musician was sitting and playing a waltz on the violin. I can't tell you how much I love waltz music, and it was absolutely right for the place.

We sat on a velvet sofa near the window, and a waiter wearing black trousers, a white shirt and a long white apron tied around his waist, came up to ask us what we'd like to order.

I asked for apple strudel, and he brought me a really large piece, with a little silver jug of cream.

Herr Heiner had a large coffee, and while he was drinking it, he talked in that warm and friendly voice of his. He said that the first day he'd met me, he'd realised that I'm a very strong-willed person, and I'd done really well at school. I'd be able to show them all back in Greece just how good I am. It'd be only one school year, it'd pass quickly, I could do additional private lessons in German, and I wouldn't lose my place in the class when I returned to Aachen.

I'd finished the second year at the German grammar school, as their primary school has only four years. In Greece I'd be in the first year at secondary school, but I'd have no difficulties, he said, as my Greek was so good. A school year passes very quickly. I'd come back and find my school in Aachen as I'd left it, and my friends too.

In the meantime, mum and dad would be able to work out their problems without stress. I had a sudden ray of hope: 'You mean, they might get back together again?' 'No, Tina, that's a fact of life, and that's the way you have to see it. During the time you're away, your parents can rebuild their lives, and as soon as you return, you'll be part of both their families, and I can assure you that then you'll be proud of yourself for having helped them.'
On the way back home, I didn't say a word. He said he understood I didn't want to talk because I needed to digest everything we'd discussed.

I was thinking that perhaps if I left, mum and dad would miss me a lot, and they'd decide that we'd all live together again, perhaps in another country – Australia for example. That's where Auntie Maria and Uncle Andreas went after they lost Venetia, and now they've adopted twins, a little boy and girl, so it's just Farmor left with her house full of Venetias.

But that idea of mine is probably rubbish. As Herr Heiner says, it's a 'fact of life' that they're splitting up, and I know that it's a 'final verdict'.

Nobody tries to tell lies to Herr Heiner, and I didn't want to let him go on believing that the reason I wasn't talking was because I was digesting what he'd told me. Actually, all I was digesting was the apple strudel, on which I'd emptied the whole silver jug of cream.

So I plucked up all my courage, and told him: 'I don't want to go anywhere,' and came close to bursting into tears.

We'd arrived just outside our house. He still had his hands on the steering wheel, and he turned and looked at me. 'On Sunday I'll come and collect you and your mum and dad, so we can go to the Roncalli Circus – they opened here yesterday.'

Sunday

Roncalli Circus. Decision.

I made my decision at the moment the ice dancer did a Lutz figure. That's a jump with a triple spin in the air, then landing on one foot on the ice.

Wednesday

Me consoling them – but I'm feeling confused.

Imagine, I had to console mum and dad because I'll be leaving soon! 'Tina, if you want you can stay and live either with your mum or with me', said dad, and hugged me so tightly I thought I'd burst. 'And Brigitte, how are you going to get on with her, then?'

But I said that just to myself. I knew that Brigitte was living on her own with her mum, who'd never married her dad. He lives in Munich, he has another family and she only sees him once a year if at all.

OK, I understand: so that Brigitte can have a dad, my dad's marrying her mum. Fine, let him have a daughter who'll look at him with dreamy eyes gazing into the distance.

I was angry, and turned my back on him. 'Don't be angry, Tina, you've no idea how your mum and I agonised over this decision, because we were thinking of you. But believe me, there was no other way.'

I don't know what to believe. It's making me even more confused to see him so sad. And to see mum looking sadder still. How could she not be – she's leaving my dad. I mean, her new guy Michalis is nice enough, quite good-looking, and he always wins at chess when he plays dad – but is that reason enough to marry him? That's why I really wanted to leave, because the more they explained it to me – mum and dad and the child psychologists and Herr Heiner – the more confused I felt. 'I'm sure you understand, Tina.' *'But didn't you notice what was going on?' 'No Farmor, not a thing.'*

From then on I didn't write anything at all in my diary.

I left.

I didn't write anything about the endless discussions. Who was going to take me to Greece? It'd have to be mum since dad couldn't leave. His school had started earlier than mum's, and he couldn't be absent on the first day of term. But poor mum was afraid Farmor would drive her mad, asking her questions about everything.

And then Tina, me, little Baby Corpse, I piped up and said: 'I'll go on my own, the same way I've been going there every year since I was five, and Farmor and the Demetrias can come and pick me up.'

Once again mum and dad hugged me tightly.

They didn't cry, though they were on the verge. Ugh! It's better not to think about it any more.

CHAPTER THREE

Before I left for Athens, they promised to come and see me for the Christmas holidays.

But they didn't come – mum, because there was a problem with Mr Michalis's baby and she couldn't travel, and dad, because out of the blue he went and broke his leg.

I was so angry. 'How on earth did you break it?' I asked him on the phone. 'It was very early in the morning, fifteen degrees below zero, I went down to the street in a hurry, I was in my slippers, hadn't put my shoes on . . . '

On a Sunday? What was my dad doing on the street early on a Sunday morning? Of course – he'd gone down to buy bread rolls. Just so Brigitte could eat bread rolls, he's sitting around at home for five weeks – plenty of time to look into her dreamy blue eyes. 'Tina, my teeny, why are you so cross that I fell over? I know, I've always told you to be careful, and now this happens to me . . . '

Laid up for five whole weeks, and then physio . . .

Just think, starting my holidays with nothing to look forward to . . . I'm coughing all the time, and this winter in Aachen was worse than any before. So no chance of them letting me come and see them over Christmas. Of course, they phone me every day. But what good is that?

If only I'd stayed in Aachen under my canopy, with my feather duvet. OK, but where would they have put Brigitte? I can't see us sleeping together in the same bed.

Dad writes that he's going to rent a large apartment, and when I go back, I'll have my own room just like before, with all my things, and mum writes – she's gone to live in the outskirts of Aachen, where Mr Michalis lives – that they'll find a place with more room, so that the baby and I can each have our own rooms.

Sigrid was right. It's no big deal. I'll have two rooms of my own and I'll celebrate my birthday twice. But what about now, while I'm stuck here in half a room, with Farmor? 'Your grandmother went through a lot', the Demetrias keep telling me. And me, haven't I gone through a lot? And aren't I still going through it?

How could I know all this was nothing compared to what was to come.

– You coming for tea?

– You coming for tea?

– You coming for tea?

– Okaayy! I was forced to reply after the third time they'd called me.

If I wasn't so mad, I'd admit that I actually enjoy it

when the Demetrias come to the house. Secretly I think of them as the three Demis.

Little Demi is very short, thin, never stands still, and interrupts Farmor when she gets onto her weird stuff.

Big Demi is wide and curvy and sweet-natured, is a bit afraid of Farmor, and keeps on saying: 'Of course, Ismeni darling, you know best.'

As for the third Demi, Smart Demi, she's the practical, positive one. Farmor says: 'Talk about getting blood from a stone – that one could get milk!' They all lived together in prison. Not that they'd killed anyone, but back then, when they were very young, during the war with the Germans, they were in the Resistance, and later they were on the Communist side during the Civil War in Greece.

Farmor decided to make me a world expert on the story of the Resistance and Grandad the Guerilla. In the ancient history we do at school, I often get mixed up about when the Hittites were in power in Asia Minor. But the period when the rebels – and my grandad – threw out the Germans and occupied Viniani and Mikro Horio, up in the Karpenissi mountains in Central Greece . . . I can reel that off by heart without even thinking.

I wonder if Farmor ever talks about anything else? At times I feel like telling her to shut up. And I do say it silently inside my head. But even if I did say it out loud, she's deaf anyway . . .

But then we fell out big time. How could Herr

Heiner have imagined he'd be the cause of all the aggro?

One day Smart Demi was quizzing me about my school in Aachen, and I began to talk about Herr Heiner, and I got all excited and started to talk more than I'd ever done before, telling them how great he was.

Suddenly I realised I was talking a lot, and I stopped.

– You can bet that the father of your wonderful Herr Heiner used to torture people in the concentration camps, said Farmor.

I lost it completely and began to shake all over.

– His father was a university lecturer, I splutter.

– So what? she replies, and carries on talking.

– Stop, Ismeni, you're just making the child confused, interrupts Little Demi.

– Since her parents haven't told her, how is she supposed to learn about it? says Farmor, and glares at me like an enemy.

I give her one of my 'dangerous looks' and decide not to tell her that everything she's mentioned I've already learnt about at school, in Aachen.

Herr Heiner used to get us together frequently, the two older classes of the primary school, and talk to us about the Second World War, and Hitler, and about the concentration camps, and about children just like us who died in the gas chambers. Last year he even told us to go and see the Italian film *Life is Beautiful*. It's about a little boy and his dad who are sent to a concentration camp in Germany. The Nazis kill the father, but not before he's managed just in the nick of time to make sure the kid will be rescued. We wrote an essay about it, and I got top marks.

But I'm not telling Farmor that. I don't want to tell her anything about our life in Aachen. I want to keep it all to myself.

I laugh a lot when I'm with the Demis. When they hark back to their time in prison, they're like young girls talking about their schooldays. Remember this? Remember that? Peals of laughter. Eventually Farmor starts laughing herself.

'Did you really all have such a great time in prison?' I asked, but Farmor gave me a dirty look, so I shut up.

It's six o'clock. Farmor asks if I've finished my homework. I don't reply, not even the third time, and I withdraw to my cage.

In Aachen this was the time I used to go out with dad for a walk on the Annastrasse.

I refuse to sit at the orange formica desk to do my homework. I fall on the bed and bury myself up to the neck under the grey blanket that makes me itch.

I want my mum. I want my dad. I want my feather duvet.

As neither mum nor dad were able to come and register me at school, it was Farmor who went with me.

From outside, the school looked like a prison, with high railings around the playground, and a big iron main gate. Scrawled on the gate in coloured paint were a load of phrases that made no sense. The only thing I could make out was a few words in white paint: COCK-A-DOODLE-DOO.

We left the yard, which to me seemed tiny, and went up to the first floor, to find the headmistress's office.

The headmistress had very dyed, very black hair with a big bun at the back, at the top of which were pinned two – definitely fake – diamond combs. Farmor explained the situation to her – that I have to stay in Greece this year for reasons of health. That's all she said, luckily.

The headmistress looks at some documents, says I've a good mark in the secondary school entrance exams, and asks about a few other things, and Farmor answers.

– You're not saying much? she asks.

Then I noticed that she was talking to me – it was probably the third time she'd asked the question.

Farmor nudged me discreetly.

I just nodded my head.

– I hope you say a bit more in class.

We left. Not a single flower in the entire playground, just hard concrete. Farmor was angry that I hadn't said anything, or asked any questions about the school. What should I have asked? What can I say? I already know I'm not going to like it.

And I didn't. The tiny classroom with its battered desks. The faded, worn-out blackboard, on which you can scarcely make out the chalked letters. Faded blue curtains hanging in tatters at the windows. I never ever go to the toilets, I hold it in until the end of school.

As for the kids, what can I say? Most of them have known one another since primary school. They came up to me all the same, asked me loads of questions . . . I didn't reply. What's the point, they're all so boring.

And the poor Greek teacher, keeping me back in the break to tell me that if I had any problems she'd help me, and I said 'No, none' and just wanted to get out of there fast.

In the playground we're so packed together that I'd rather stay in the classroom for break if I was allowed to. Outside there isn't even the smallest bench to sit down on; or rather, there is one, but it's lost all its wooden bits, so it looks like an iron skeleton.

I park myself in a corner, by the wall. A short while later, a young girl comes and stands next to me.

– You also are alien? Me – Russia.

Well, naturally I realise that I speak – when I speak at all – a bit differently from the other kids. It's not that I have an accent, but they use words I never say, and don't even understand.

So now, what am I to say to this girl, who puts her warm little hand in mine? I don't say anything, but

I leave my hand in hers.

– You have beautiful eyes.

I look at her in surprise.

She's called Tamara. Her mum works as a cleaner at the school, but she used to be a pharmacist where they came from, and her dad was a physics teacher – now he paints houses. If we want, she says, maybe he'll paint ours for nothing. They were starving back where they were, that's why they left.

'Farmor, they're all starving in your wonderful Russia!' I'm so looking forward to running home and telling her that. But what am I going to do about Tamara, who's expecting me to tell her all about myself?

Luckily the bell rang.

I'm top of the class at maths. I'm much more advanced than anyone else in the class, because what they've just started on, I did last year.

Our teacher, Mr Benos, is very young, handsome, tall, rather pale, with wavy hair and blue eyes – just as I imagine angels look like – and he never has a go at me. The kids say he sings really beautifully, they've heard him at school fetes. He's supposed to be even better than some pop singer they call Kouvas or Rouvas – I didn't catch the name properly – and all the girls are in love with him.

– Mr Benos, why don't you become a pop singer? Vicky asks him: a tall girl, average pupil, but not afraid of anything or anybody – not even of the headmistress.

– Because I like what I do, replies Mr Benos.

– D'you realise how mega-rich he could be?

Vicky was going on and on about it during break.

– For now he has to make do with that scooter that looks as if it might fall to pieces any moment. My father asked him to give me private lessons, but he wouldn't hear of it. Pity, because I like him a lot. If he became another Rouvas, I'd go absolutely wild.

I saw him once on TV, this Kouvas, sorry, Rouvas, and I can't see what they're making all the fuss about.

But then I went crazy over Leonardo di Caprio, the actor who was in *Titanic*, and I saw the film three times with Sigrid, and we cried over Leonardo all three times, when he was swallowed up by the waves. I'd filled my room up with posters of him. I was all of ten years old back then. Last year, though, when I turned twelve, I threw them all out and put up my lovely horse again, and a really beautifully ugly goggle-eyed frog. And then, when I was with Sigrid and we saw di Caprio on the cover of some magazine, we were both baffled that we'd liked him so much . . . Shame about all those tears we'd shed for him.

Mr Benos used to get me to come up to the blackboard all the time – he'd tell me not to slouch, and was amazed at how much maths I already knew.

I'd vowed to myself to keep my promise to Herr Heiner, to become, if not first in the class, at least second.

But I didn't keep my promise. I couldn't. Perhaps it was the hamster's fault, or rather, the excursion to Karpenissi.

I came back from school deep in thought. At break a boy from the third year had come over and talked to me.

I remembered Vicky's suggestion: 'If you want us to find some boys who are cool, we should chat up some of the Third Years.'

Truth is, our classmates seem like babies. Boys with red chubby cheeks and spots, others whose heads only just come up to our shoulders. And I had no interest at all in meeting boys, even ones from Year Three. Anyway, when a tall, slim, pale-faced boy came up to me, out of the corner of my eye I saw Vicky signalling 'No!' But before I had any idea why, he began to talk to me.

He'd heard I'd been in Germany. He'd come from there himself last year.

– How are you getting on? he asked.

– OK, I answered briefly.

He said he was having a really bad time. He'd come back to Athens with his mum, because his parents had divorced and his dad was staying on in Germany. They'd been living in Cologne, he was going to a music school there and wanted to carry on with it, but his dad had started another family and hadn't any room for him. His mother, on the other hand, wanted to come back to Greece, to be with her parents.

Cologne! Only an hour by train from Aachen. I often went there with mum and dad, because we had friends there.

– I used to live in Aachen.

– I know, he said. I was surprised he knew that, too.

He'd often been to concerts there with his class and music teachers.

– Look, he said, and showed me a little silver animal hanging round his neck on a black leather thong.

It was the wolf from the Cathedral with the hole in his middle, where the Devil had taken his soul.

– Poor old wolf, they really made a fool of him, I said, just to say something.

– They're making fools of us, too.

I stepped back so as to take a good look at him. I had to crane my neck, because he was much taller than me. His eyes were a strange golden colour, one of them a bit darker than the other. I guessed his hair must be golden-blond too, if it weren't so unwashed, matted and greasy.

– We couldn't bring the piano. Mum says I'll just have to practise on my computer keyboard.

He wanted to tell me more, but I could sense Vicky staring at me, and I told him my friend was waiting. I left him standing on his own in the middle of the school yard.

He reminded me of someone, with those long thin legs, and his hands dangling loose by his side. I didn't need to look round for Vicky. She ran up to me, to ask what he'd said to me, and to warn me to be careful.

– He's weird. He never talks to any of the kids, so I'm wondering what he wants with you. His schoolwork is appalling, and he skives off all the time.

I didn't know what 'skive' meant, but I didn't ask her to explain.

I have no problems in understanding the Greek teacher, same with Mr Benos. It's only the kids. 'Skive', hmm! I'll ask Smart Demi to tell me. She knows everything. She studied all the time she was in prison, and by the time she came out, she was a wise woman.

On the way home, I was wondering who it was that boy reminded me of, and suddenly I knew. It was Wick, Pinocchio's friend, with the lick of hair sticking up like a candlewick; the lazy, dreamy boy who eventually gets turned into a donkey.

While the Demis were shifting Farmor's stuff to get my room sorted, a book had fallen out of a cardboard box. I picked it up and opened it out of curiosity. On the flyleaf were the words: 'To my dear Venetia, with love from her Granny'.

I hid it under my shirt, and later, once my 'cage' was ready, I went in and looked at the book in peace. It was *Pinocchio*. I'd already read it in German. I began to browse through it. Somehow it seemed much more fun in Greek. There was one whole-page drawing of a thin boy with tousled hair and at the bottom was his name: Wick. The spitting image of the boy who'd talked to me at break.

I reached Kypseli Square, and as soon as I turned the corner to get home, I noticed the shop which has puppies in the window and birdcages hanging outside. I forgot about Wick, and just stood there, idly gawping. Then I saw that next to the window with the puppy dogs, in another, smaller window there was a cage of hamsters. My heart began to race . . .

So what has become of my Leonardo di Caprio? Is he nuzzling Brigitte's fingers with his little snout, while she rests her hand on the the rails of his cage? Surely not! It's me he knows, and these little animals are very timid, they don't go to just anybody. I'd intended to change his name, when I stopped liking di Caprio. But then I thought, it's not the hamster's fault, is it?

I went into the shop and asked how much the hamsters cost. Mum and dad send me quite a lot of pocket money. Farmor gets worked up about it, but it's OK, she lets me keep it. Only problem was, I didn't have any money with me.

I dashed home, dropped my schoolbag and went out again like a whirlwind, saying I was going to buy something. Farmor didn't say anything. She thought I needed an exercise book or something else for school.

I went back to the shop, asked to look at the hamsters, and grabbed hold of a reddish blond one. It was staring directly at me with its beady eyes. 'Hello, Herr Heiner,' I said to myself, and I felt its little body warming my hand.

I bought it. I bought a yellow cage as well, with a wheel for it to do its exercises, and I got some food for it, and carried it proudly home.

– What's that? asked Farmor, as if she'd never seen a hamster before in her life.

– Let me introduce you to Herr Heiner.

She looked at me with her mouth open, then she began to shriek. On and on about how I do whatever I want without asking her, I bring rats into the house, and she's going to tell them to cut off my pocket money. She was blocking the front door so I couldn't get in.

– Take it back immediately!

– No!

I must have said it quite ferociously, and without thinking I made a sidestep and slipped past her into the house, ran into my room, slammed the door – and I'd have locked it, too, if Farmor hadn't taken away the key the moment the room had become mine. In a trice she'd jerked the door open, as she always did.

I was sitting on the bed with my arms round the cage.

She went on and on about how selfish I was. Children were dying of hunger, but instead of helping them I just buy rats.

I couldn't get any words out. I sat totally still, with the cage on my knees. Herr Heiner had hidden himself deep inside his little hutch.

Farmor turned her back on me and left the room. I just knew she'd go and telephone dad. I heard her dial a long number – right, she was calling him on her mobile . . . Occasional words reached my ears. They felt like stones hitting me.

– You've brought her up badly . . . she doesn't listen . . . she doesn't ask me permission . . . yes, a rat, I'm telling you . . . Aha, she had one there? . . . I don't want it . . . it's a matter of principle. Now tell me about your leg . . . No more evading the issue – when will you be giving up that crutch?

Then I think she must have realised I was listening and closed the living room door.

I got up and looked around the room for a place to put the cage. I pushed everything aside that was on my desk and stood the cage on it – there was nowhere else. I'd just have to read in bed and write with the books propped on my knees.

I can tell, Herr Heiner doesn't like noise, and it'd disturb him if I was scribbling on paper and turning pages right next to him.

It's a shame the Demetrias aren't coming today. Maybe Little Demi would take my side.

We ate without speaking. Farmor had her lips pressed tightly together. If there's one thing I can't stand about people, it's when they sulk.

– You know, Farmor, they're very quiet little creatures, and I'll take care of it. I had one in Aachen, I said in the sweetest tone I could manage.

Farmor didn't reply, but just pressed her lips together even more, so that her mouth disappeared.

Then I grabbed the heart of the lettuce from the middle of the salad, because I knew how much Herr Heiner would enjoy it, and I got up really quickly from the table to go and feed it to him. I thought I'd got rid of her, because she didn't follow me straight away. But while Herr Heiner was nibbling his lettuce outside his little hutch, and I was sitting on my bed with my homework on my lap, Farmor burst in without knocking.

She really lost it when she saw what I was doing, and stood there speechless for a moment. Then her eyes flashed angrily, the way they do when she talks about the fascists, and she spoke in a way that forbids any more discussion.

– You'll take that animal back tomorrow. I won't have you becoming a complete hunchback, doing your homework in that position.

She went out and slammed the door shut. However strange it sounds, I felt happy, because I could see how upset she was that I might develop a hunched back. Was it possible she actually cared about me a little? She's never called me 'My dear Tina'. The 'my dear' was only for Venetia. Maybe if I was nicer to her, she'd let me keep the hamster? Should I get up early tomorrow morning and go and buy her newspaper before going to school, and leave it on the table for her to find? When I go to buy something from the kiosk and I'm in a bad mood, I pretend I've forgotten to buy her newspaper. It winds her up. She says I only ever think of myself, then she has to go out and buy it herself.

So tomorrow I'll fetch it really early in the morning and I'll even tell her: 'Farmor, I do actually know the names of the two men from the Resistance who tore down the swastika flag from the Acropolis during the

German Occupation.'

Of course I know. She's told me a hundred times, it was Glezos and Santas, natch. We've even learnt about it in school; but when she checks to see if I've finally got it, and I'm in a ratty mood, either I tell her it was Kolokotronis – the hero of the 1821 uprising against the Turks, ha ha! – or just to get her really mad, I say it was Captain Corelli.

What a lovely sleep I had that night! In my sleep I could hear Herr Heiner turning his exercise wheel – he only comes out of his hutch when it's dark – and I felt I had some company. And then I dreamt about the real Herr Heiner, how he'd come to our home in Aachen to discuss things with my mum and dad.

I woke up and hurried out to buy Farmor's newspaper.

She didn't fall for it though.

– As soon as you get back from school, you'll take that animal back to the shop.

Before leaving, I went to my room and said to Herr Heiner:

– Don't worry, I won't take you back. I'll make such a fuss . . .

Even when I want to be nice to her, Farmor won't let me. And yet she cared about me hunching my back! . . .

But I didn't need to make a fuss. The Demetrias came to the rescue and saved Herr Heiner.

CHAPTER FOUR

It was nearly the end of February, and there was so much sunshine – more than we ever saw in Aachen, even in the summer.

Farmor and the Demis decided we'd have a week-end excursion to Karpenissi. Little Demi has a tiny car. She was at the steering wheel, Farmor beside her. The two other Demis squeezed into the back, with me in the middle, playing constantly with my game boy. Though I'd switched off the sound, they were all getting irritated, even Little Demi, who's usually my counsel for the defence.

– Don't you want to look out the window? Look how lovely it all is.

– Well now you'll have to take a look, we're going to stop here for a while.

– The whole story of your grandad is engraved on this spot.

I knew the story. Every summer that Farmor had taken me to Karpenissi, we'd stop at the same place and they'd tell me all over again. I can't say I remembered much of it, because I was usually too busy catching a ladybird so I could make it crawl over my fingers.

Farmor and her three friends got out of the car. I lagged behind a bit, because I wanted to catch the monster I was chasing on the game boy.

Little Demi pulled me out before Farmor noticed I hadn't left the car. Then I saw that the four of them were forming a semi-circle as if they were about to take part in a play, standing there just like the actors in the ancient theatre at Epidaurus that I'd seen last year.

Last year at Epidaurus! I'd gone with mum and Herr Heiner, who was spending his holidays in Greece. Dad said he would be coming later on, as he was finishing a course, but he called us up all the time and said 'I'm missing you'. *'So you didn't notice anything at all?' 'No, Farmor, not a thing.'*

Little Demi stepped forwards out of the little circle they'd formed, as if she was going to recite something:

– It was here.

– No, a bit more over that way, said Big Demi.

– Here, here, just before that little bend in the road, said Farmor.

Smart Demi took a pace forwards and then turned in a circle all around the same spot.

– This is where I was standing, right in the middle of the road, waving with both hands. Didn't raise them too high though, because I was afraid the pillow I'd fastened round my stomach might fall down.

Then they began to speak quickly, one after the other.

– We'd got inside information. That the lorry transferring him would pass this spot.

– It arrived bang on time.

– He was in the back of the lorry, with just one German soldier guarding him. It was spring, remember? Flowers everywhere. At the front, in the cab, there was another soldier next to the driver.

– The lorry stopped as soon as they saw me. The co-driver got out. I knew a bit of German. I said I'd started having contractions, could they take me to Lamia. They were talking it over amongst themselves, when suddenly resistance fighters sprang out from the forest and took them by surprise. The Germans didn't even manage to get to their weapons. The guerillas clambered into the lorry, shot the guard and the driver, and tied up the other soldier. And you, Ismeni, you got up into the lorry and threw your arms round Konstantinos. You found the keys in the guard's pocket and unlocked his handcuffs. And we all vanished just as we'd come, back into the forest.

Smart Demi told us the whole story with a far-off look, as if she was at the cinema and the images were passing before her eyes, and she was just retelling what she was looking at on the screen.

– It was your granny who organised the whole thing, said Big Demi, who always said least of all. She did it to save your grandad from the clutches of the Germans.

Farmor didn't say anything. She got into the car and we followed her. Until we got to Karpenissi none of them spoke at all, and I didn't dare play with my game boy. All I was worrying about was whether I'd left enough food for Herr Heiner.

We weren't staying at Karpenissi itself, but a bit further up, in Mikro Horio, where Big Demi has a beautiful little house with a garden. Farmor's family house in Karpenissi was sold off when times got hard, just so they could survive. Countless times we've driven by and she's pointed it out to me. It's a two-storeyed house with a wide balcony. These days, there's a sign that takes up the whole front of the balcony, that says: INSTITUTE OF ENGLISH LANGUAGE.

So whenever we went to Karpenissi, we stayed at Big Demi's little house. Farmor and her three mates would sleep in the bedroom, and I'd have the couch in the living room, which was lovely and warm, with a big stove burning day and night. And best of all, I could cover myself with a proper quilt, not quite the same as the feather bed I had in Aachen, but at least there wasn't a sheet falling off me or blankets making me itch.

I love Mikro Horio although there isn't any sea, and I'm mad about the sea. But just up the road there's the waterfall at Proussos, and when I go to stay for a week or so in the summer, I splash about with the other kids in the cold water. There are no kids at this time of the year though. All the people who used to live in Mikro Horio left a long time ago and went to live in Athens or somewhere else. But in the summer some kids come for holidays and there are a few grans and grandads who've stayed on and who invite their grandchildren.

The first day was quite OK. Big Demi had told Magdalena, who looks after the house, to light the big stove, and Little Demi immediately put some chestnuts on the hob. They split as they roasted, and we ate them hot.

We had a visitor in the early evening, a wizened old man. Farmor and her three mates made a big fuss of Captain Trap, as they called him. But he was really pleased to see them too: He kept on saying: 'Hey, hey, the girls are back!'

He ate with us and then he asked them:

– So how are things then?

– Terrible, replied Farmor.

– No, no, Ismeni, they certainly aren't terrible, said Little Demi.

– I'll go and get some bedding for Tina, said Big Demi, who saw I was yawning.

She made my bed on the couch. I went into the room where I'd left my rucksack, and pulled on my pyjamas in the freezing cold, then raced back into the living room to dive down under the bedclothes. Big Demi switched off my light next to the couch and went back to join the others who were still sitting round the table, talking in low voices.

I enjoyed that. It's just like when I hear Herr Heiner whirring his wheel round in the middle of the night.

The logs were crackling in the stove, and Captain Trap was telling a story from his wartime past as if it was a fairy tale, and every now and then he'd raise his voice: '. . . and it was there that I caught the Germans in my TRRAPP!! . . .'

All hell broke loose next morning in Viniani, and it was all over a horse and a pair of shoelaces.

Farmor and the three Demis insisted we should go to Viniani, though it was quite a long way. They wanted to see if the building works had finished on the old school, which was being turned into a Museum of the Resistance.

On the way the four of them sang rebel songs, just like girls on a school trip. I'd put my headphones on and I was listening to my CD – the one with my favourite group, Silver Moon.

I realised the car had stopped, but I must have missed what they were trying to tell me, as I still had my headphones on. Farmor pulled them off.

– When you have that thing on, it's as if you're deaf and dumb. The way it's going, soon we'll have to communicate in sign language.

I didn't bother to reply, just got out of the car with the others, dragging my feet in a bored sort of way. They headed for the school, and I dawdled behind them.

Farmor turned and looked at me, or rather she looked at my feet.

– Tie up your shoelaces, you'll fall over.

I was expecting her to say it three times, so I could reply:

– I don't have any shoelaces.

– What do you mean you don't have any shoelaces? How come you've no shoelaces? Why don't you have shoelaces? What did you do with your shoelaces? What did you do with your shoelaces? What did you DO with your SHOELACES?

I said I'd no idea where they were. Probably in Aachen.

She called the others over, forgot all about the school and whether the building works were finished, and she asked them if they'd ever seen anyone wearing shoes without laces.

No, they hadn't.

'Well, you can see it now', I said, silently to myself.

Luckily, Big Demi changed the subject, and they stopped going on about the laces.

– I can remember this school at the time of the Occupation. This was the headquarters of the Resistance. No German dared to set foot anywhere in the whole of this mountain region of Eurytania.

And once more I had the impression from the way she was speaking, it was as if she was watching a film unfolding before her eyes.

Suddenly, while she was in mid-film, my eye was caught by a horse grazing in a field nearby. I ran over to it.

It was jet black, like Diagora. Its eyes were glistening and gentle, like his. I went up close and stroked its mane, just as Brigitte had shown me. He bent his head down and leant it against my cheek.

I heard steps. A tall, slim lad appeared. As soon as he saw me, he smiled.

– I can see Black Beauty liked you straight away.

Then the boy asked me how I came to be there, and I told him I'd come with my gran and her friends to see the school.

I turned and looked round for them, but they were a long way off.

– Do you want to ride him? He's very tame.

Before I managed to get an answer out, he threw a sack that he'd been holding in his hands over the horse's back. My heart was pounding so much I thought it would burst. The boy clasped the fingers of both his hands together and told me to step on them, so I could get up. Oh well, I'd not be going far, just a little ride around. There weren't any reins so I wouldn't be able to go very fast. I didn't need to think about it twice, I stepped up on his hands and got on. I hadn't imagined he'd have such strong hands.

The boy slapped the horse two or three times on its back, and very gently, stepping out lightly, the horse walked me as far as the school enclosure. I was sitting with my back absolutely straight, practising my balance. Then I leant down and hugged his hot neck tightly.

Just then, as I was bent forwards, I saw them coming out of the school. The three Demis and Farmor remained motionless, watching me.

I hugged the horse even more tightly round the neck.

Farmor opened her mouth, but no words came out. Then she suddenly caught sight of the boy.

– Did you put her up there?

– He's a really tame pony, he said defensively.

She came up to me, caught hold of my leg and pulled at it.

The boy moved right in front of her.

– 'You'll make her fall off like that. I'll get her down.

Again he twined his fingers together, I stepped on them and got down. He went off, and the horse followed him. I didn't even manage to thank them both.

Oh, I'd really done it this time. They'd driven all this way so I could see the living breathing history of Greece! OK, we'd come in the summer the year before last, but I was young and didn't understand much, and the school wasn't a museum then. But now it was, and I hadn't even gone inside to find out who I had to thank for being able to live in freedom today!

'What freedom?' I said to myself.

They went back into the museum with me. The Demis were talking, talking, only Farmor wasn't saying anything. She had those tightly pressed lips, like when she's lost her temper, and her mouth had vanished again.

I couldn't concentrate on anything they were saying, all I could feel was her icy stare. But I felt better when I glimpsed the black horse turning towards me on the other side of the meadow, as if trying to catch sight of me.

Even when we got home, they didn't speak to me at all. Captain Trap didn't come to tell his tales that evening. They made up my bed on the couch, and as soon as we'd eaten, I went to lie down.

I couldn't get to sleep, but I pretended to. I couldn't imagine they'd spend the whole time talking about shoelaces! They weren't talking about the Germans or the Resistance, they weren't going on about their time in prison or exile. Nothing about all that – just shoelaces.

Farmor was saying that it was all my parents' fault, they let me traipse about like that. Big Demi said she thought it might be a fashion, because she remembered having seen one of her great-nephews wearing shapeless trainers without shoelaces, but she hadn't paid much attention at the time.

– A fashion? Little Demi was totally amazed.

And then she began to tell how when she was sixteen, in Peristeri – the working-class suburb where she lived with her parents – she used to have to walk around barefoot. Even in the harsh, cold, wartime winters, during the hungry times of the Occupation. A cousin of hers gave her a pair of shoes, which had got too small for him. It didn't matter to her that they were boys' shoes, or that they were old and worn out. But she was ashamed that they had no laces. Her mother looked and looked, but couldn't find any laces anywhere. You'd think shoelaces had disappeared together with the food supplies.

– Just imagine . . . I was starving, I was freezing, and all I was crying over was shoelaces!

Then they started to talk more quietly, and I couldn't hear what they were saying. I got down under the quilt and wanted to cry, and then to laugh, that shoelaces had suddenly become such a big deal.

I didn't cry, I didn't laugh. I fell asleep.

When I woke up the following morning, there was no sign of them having their coffee.

I got up. On the table, there was just a bowl and next to it a jugful of milk and the cereal box. Next to it, a note:

Konstantina,

Captain Trap has fallen ill and we're taking him to the doctor in Karpenissi. If he needs to go to hospital, we could be a long time. At lunchtime Magdalena will bring you some moussaka. If you go for a walk in the square, go out by the back door and leave the key in the flower-pot.

Take care

Farmor

– Yeeeeeeees!

I tossed the note high up in the air. I was on my own until lunchtime, maybe even later. It wasn't that I wanted Captain Trap to be really ill, but where would I get such an opportunity again?

In Athens, Farmor (it's true, she's actually written 'Farmor' in her note, the first time she's officially acknowledged the name I've given her) used to leave the house only when I was at school or at my German class. She's never given me the key to the house (in Aachen I'd had a key from the time I was eight) and she was always home when I got back. Now for the very first and only time, she wouldn't be watching me. I could eat my cereal with cold milk, the way I like it, without Farmor telling me that milk straight from the fridge is bad for you.

In Aachen, we all drank milk from the fridge. I was almost on my way to the kitchen to fetch it, when what did I see – right in front of me, perched on top of the cereal box – but a pair of shoelaces! I picked them up, lit the stove and hurled them into it. What was Farmor thinking? That as soon as I saw them, I'd lace up my shoes and go 'boo-hoo' like Little Demi, because poor me, I didn't have any shoelaces? I was the one who pulled out the laces after I'd bought my boots.

Doesn't she understand anything about kids today? She doesn't seem to have any idea about yesterday's kids either; I can just imagine what my poor dad went through when he was little, even though he's never mentioned it. Poor old dad! As soon as I've finished my breakfast, I'm going to make a beeline for the square. Yesterday, I noticed there's a telephone box that works with phone cards. I'll buy a card from the kiosk. At home, Farmor's always standing next to me when I phone, and I never thought before of phoning mum and dad from a telephone box. They'd have thought it strange. But here Big Demi doesn't have a phone.

I went to the kitchen, fetched the bottle of cold milk from the fridge, and for the first time since I left Aachen I actually enjoyed my cereal. Then I poured the milk Farmor had left me in the jug back into the bottle. I cleared the table straight away; they normally have to ask me three times before I do it. Then I got dressed, put on my jacket and left by the back door. I put the key in the flower-pot and dashed along the lanes of Mikro Horio.

The square wasn't far from the house. Soon I'd be speaking to them. It was Sunday, and still quite early. I'd find each of them at home. Either they'd both answer the phone themselves or I'd get Mr Michalis and Frau Sabrina. That wouldn't matter, I'd just ask to speak to mum or dad.

My heart was beating wildly as I slipped the card into the telephone . . . What if I started to cry? I was so excited I dialled the wrong number, and a voice I didn't know answered. I said sorry, and put the phone down.

While I was preparing to dial again, I could hear someone standing right behind me, speaking German. I turned round in surprise. It was a young man who looked like a tourist, with a rucksack on his back. He'd heard me speaking German, and asked me if I knew which direction they should take for the waterfall at Proussos. I said I knew the way, and he called over to a girl who was sitting nearby at a table drinking coffee. She came up to where we were standing. She was very blonde, with a freckled face, and she was slim – quite skinny in fact. She was wearing a pair of frayed blue jeans, and a very white pullover, very short and tight – you could see her belly button where a ring with a red jewel was sparkling in the sunlight. I was always dreaming of piercing my belly button and putting in a ring just like it.

Of course, mum and dad wouldn't let me. They said I'd have to get a bit older first. Well, now I am older and one day I'll pierce it myself – I know you put ice on the spot where you want the hole, and then heat up the needle, and the prick doesn't hurt at all.

That's how I did the second hole in my ear. And Farmor really freaked about that second hole – I can't understand why one hole doesn't matter, but two are something terrible. If I do decide to go ahead and have a piercing in my belly button, then Farmor will go absolutely ape – the fuss she kicked up about a couple of shoelaces will be nothing by comparison!

– Well, will you show us the way? the German boy asked.

I turned and looked at him. His hair was blond, really blond, and he was wearing a black leather jacket. He was really good-looking, and he had a single ring in one ear, with what looked like a real diamond.

I fell into a daze while I was looking at him. And when he asked me again if I could show them the way to Proussos, I thought, why not? I'm free, I can do whatever I want, and I forgot all about the phone and everything else. I just knew I was free for half a day. Captain Trap just needed to be a little bit sicker and they'd be held up for even longer.

So I suggested to the Germans that I could go with them, if they weren't going to come back too late. They were all for it. A bit further down from the square, they'd parked a large black jeep laden with rucksacks. The girl sat at the wheel and put me next to her. The young man asked me how it was I could speak German so well. I told him I'd lived in Aachen. So then they both raised their little fingers, I raised mine, and we had to laugh . . . for that's the traditional greeting in Aachen.

A short distance from our house in Aachen, there's actually a bronze sculpture of little children smiling and lifting their little fingers.

And whenever mum and dad left the house on their own to go somewhere, I'd stand at the window, watching. They always turned their heads to look up at me, and then I'd lift up my little finger. They'd lift theirs in return, smiling up at me.

Neither the young man nor the girl asked me any more questions. That's the way the Germans are. If you want to tell them something, you say it. Otherwise, they don't ask. Not like here, where they all drive me mad – the grown-ups as well as the kids. Why did I go to Germany? . . . Why did I come back? . . . What does my mum do? . . . What does my dad do? . . . Why do I live with my gran? . . .

When I told Farmor that the Germans don't ask questions, she snapped back: 'And that's why they got saddled with Hitler – because they don't ask any questions.'

Honestly, how can she possibly still hate them – it's so many years since the Second World War!

So there I was, careering towards Proussos with Farmor's deadly enemies, and I felt really happy and free. So free, that it didn't matter to me any more whether Captain Trap might have just a minor complaint, and they'd soon come home and find me missing.

I turned my head to show the young man a great view of the mountainside we'd just passed, and I noticed his hands were shaking. Who knows what was wrong with him? I guessed that was why he wasn't doing the driving. We reached a sign and I told them we couldn't go any further in the car. We left it by the side of the road, and took the footpath uphill to Proussos.

I was walking on ahead, scrambling up the paths like a mountain goat. The girl was following me, and behind us the young man, puffing and panting to keep up.

'D'you want to stop?' I asked.

'Jan?' The girl turned round and looked at him.

'Two minutes,' he said. 'I'll be fine in just a mo.'

We stopped. Jan, as the girl had called him, took a little box out of his pocket, picked out two small pills, and put them in his mouth. Then he unhooked a flask fastened to his belt, drank down several gulps of water, closed his eyes for a few seconds, and then opened them again.

'Problem solved. Now we can go on.'

I was afraid he might be ill, but as we walked on he became more and more lively, and just before we reached the waterfall he began to whistle. After we'd climbed a path going up the mountain, we heard the noise of the waterfall, and in a short while we saw Proussos right in front of us.

Jan and the girl began to get undressed – she got down to her bright red pants, and Jan was in a pair of black briefs. There wasn't anyone else there except us. I could see the water must be very cold, because they shrieked as soon as they jumped in, then almost immediately they waded along to the spot beneath the waterfall and began to play around, shouting and laughing. I was left there, gawping at them.

– Come in, come in, they shouted to me, but I could scarcely make out what they were saying with the noise of the water.

'Come in, come in' – the waterfall was inviting me in too, knowing how I used to splash around in the waters during the summer, and once again I felt cold. Jan made a funnel with his hand so I could hear.

– Don't be afraid, he shouted up to me.

I wasn't afraid. Mum's always saying how fearless I am. Whenever we go to the big swimming pool, I always dive in from the high board, while she's quite timid and always jumps off the lowest one.

I wasn't afraid of the waterfall, I just didn't want to strip off. I took off my jacket and pullover and ran up to the water's edge in my shirt and jeans. I didn't even think about how I was going to manage afterwards. After all, I was free for half a day wasn't I? I plunged into the waterfall. It took my breath away, the water was absolutely freezing, and falling with enormous force.

Jan and the girl gave me their hands so I wouldn't slip, but as I knew every single stone, I could stand firm.

As the water fell, it seemed to be getting warmer, and washing all my cares away.

The two of them obviously felt the same, because they started singing. As soon as they'd finished, they caught hold of my hands and lifted me almost into the air, then we got out of the water and sat on the stones, which were hot from the sun.

The girl got a towel out of her bag and gave it to Jan so he could dry himself.

Then they both took off their wet things right there in front of me, dried themselves off, and put on dry clothes.

I was shivering, although I was sitting in the sun. The girl searched in her bag and found a coloured sarong, just a piece of cloth, really. She told me to take off my wet jeans and shirt, and wear the cloth as a skirt. I took it, but I didn't want to get undressed in front of them, so I went behind a rock. I stripped off, dried my dripping hair as well as I could with my wet shirt, then I wrapped the sarong around me, and put on my pullover and my jacket as well. I sat down in the sun and felt really great.

The other two were lying in the sun with their eyes closed.

We drove back to Mikro Horio and sat at the café in the main square. Jan ordered three brandies. I was wondering who the third one was for. When the waiter brought them Jan picked up one of the glasses and gave it to me.

– Just drink it down all at once. That way you won't get a chill.

Well, why shouldn't I drink it? I'm free to do what I want, aren't I? I did as they did, emptying the glass in one gulp. I felt as if I was on fire, and my eyes were watering, but soon a gentle warmth wrapped itself round my whole body. I offered to go home and change and bring the sarong back, but the girl shook her head.

– It's old, you can throw it away.

The clock in the square struck twice, and I was suddenly so scared, Jan and his girlfriend both noticed. He held my hand.

– Are you frightened you'll be in trouble?

I didn't reply, but I felt all the blood running out of my veins, and my hand was trembling in his. Then he opened his bag, took out the little box with the pills, picked one out and offered it to me. The girl stopped him.

– Leave it out, he said, pulling his hand away from under hers – it'll do her good, and then she won't be so stressed.

I believed him, because I'd seen what a terrible

state he'd been in, and how much better he was as soon as he'd taken the pills.

He put it in my hand and I swallowed it down quickly with a gulp of water.

They thanked me as I said goodbye, then I ran off back to the house without bothering to use the phone box. I told myself I'd phone my parents later that evening.

I was completely out of breath by the time I reached the house. They weren't back, the key was still in the flower-pot, and I went in quickly to get changed.

But what could I put on? I'd brought a clean T-shirt with me, but no spare jeans. I hung my wet ones out to dry in the courtyard, but even in the sun they'd take a long time. So I stayed in the sarong, and wondered what excuse I could give Farmor and the Demetrias.

Clackety-clack, the sound of their footsteps outside the door, and suddenly I wasn't frightened any more. I felt happy and weightless, as if I might take off and fly.

They came up and caught sight of me sitting on the stone bench in front of the house, swinging my legs to and fro. I raised my little finger to greet them in the good old Aachen way.

– Have you hurt your finger? asked Farmor.

– No – that's just the way they say hello in Aachen, I replied laughing.

Little Demi laughed too.

– That's nice, as we can't give the clenched fist

salute any more, we can raise our little fingers.

– Just what we needed, said Smart Demi.

Then the four of them noticed my jeans fluttering in the breeze.

– Why are your jeans on the line?

– Have you been washing them?

– Where did you get them dirty?

– What's that scrap of cloth you're wearing?

So then Tina, me that is (but it wasn't me at all, more as if I'd left my body and I was someone else, and this other person jumped down off the stone bench and went to stand right in front of Farmor and the three Demis), this other Tina picked up the sarong that had fallen off and was trailing on the ground, she stretched her head, for it seemed to her that birds were flying high up in the sky, lifted her arms as if she wanted to touch them, and said in a happy-go-lucky voice:

– I went to Proussos.

– To Proussos?

– Proussos?

– Proussos?

– You went to Proussos?

Four different voices – anxious, amazed, astonished, angry.

But Tina wasn't bothered at all. She was staring at the birds and reaching up on tiptoe to catch hold of them, and she didn't even wait for them to say it three times before responding.

– Yes, to Proussos.

– How did you get there?

– Who with?
– Did you slip and fall in?
– Did you get wet?
– No, I didn't fall in, I went in.
– You went in?
– Went in?
– Went in?
– Went in?
– Yup, I went in.

All four of them, one after the other, just like a chorus. But nothing seems to bother this Tina. She looks at them smiling and she's secretly glad they're so terrified.

– I found a German couple in the square, who wanted to go to Proussos. They took me along with them. It was fantastic . . .

She's overdoing it, this Tina. It's time to rein her in. The little pill that Jan gave me seems to have worked like magic. Of course, that's what must have done it: for when he was in such bad shape, he'd taken the pills and in a short while he was fine. 'Time to go back inside, Tina', I tell her, and she went back into my body.

– Don't worry, Farmor, I won't catch cold, I drank some brandy and got warmed up again', I said, with the sweetest voice I could manage.

It wasn't Farmor who gave me the slap, but Smart Demi. It didn't hurt at all.

– You beat me to it, Farmor said to her. She was shaking from head to toe, and the others took her into the house.

In the evening we left for Athens. I didn't listen to what they said in the car, as I kept my headphones on, and turned up Silver Moon. I kept up the rhythm, beating my hand on my leg. But suddenly I felt my hand shaking, as if the fearless Tina had left me, and taken all the fun and laughter with her. The music was getting all mixed up and my head was buzzing. I took off the headphones and closed my eyes.

– Are you all right? I heard Big Demi's voice from a long way off, just as I fell asleep.

CHAPTER FIVE

I woke up once we reached Kypseli. Farmor and I got out of the car.

I can see us both back home. Farmor's absolutely fine, wide awake, bolt upright, while I'm feeling terrible, dragging the sarong on the floor, longing to hear the voices of my mum and dad.

– Let's phone them, I mumbled.

– Of course we're going to phone them, said Farmor with her stern voice.

But she sent me off to have a hot bath first, because she had 'no wish for me to get bronchitis on top of everything else'.

In Aachen we had really big bath towels which I used to wrap all around me. There was one I particularly liked, dazzling white, with two large storks.

Here Farmor gives me two towels – they're scarcely bigger than face towels. One is for my body, one for my legs, and it makes me cross that I keep mixing them up.

Somehow, with the coupons she collects from the newspapers, she'd got hold of two towelling bathrobes, one pink and one blue. She showed them off proudly to the Demis, then she put them in one of the cardboard boxes in her room. I could never work out what she was going to do with all that stuff she was collecting with the coupons. Frying pans, quilts, sheets, toasters, even a whole box full of pliers and screwdrivers.

I never dared ask her, then one day I saw the Demetrias arriving and loading up the tiny old banger. So I asked Little Demi:

– Where are you going?

– To the Kurds, she replied.

I'd often heard them talking about the Kurdish refugees with Farmor, and what a miserable life they were living in warehouses and cellars. I've no problem with the Kurds, but I was outraged that the Kurdish kids would be drying themselves on the pink and blue towelling robes, while here's me trying to dry myself on these lousy little hand towels.

I felt more of a wet rag than the sarong. Why hadn't Jan given me more of those amazing little pills, so I could take one now? I don't even know what they were called, so I can't ask for them at the chemist's. I just remember they were a sky-blue colour.

Going into the dining room, I heard Farmor's voice. She was speaking angrily into the phone. As soon as I came over, she handed me the receiver.

It was dad. As soon as I heard his voice I began to cry, but as he went on I calmed down.

– In the summer you'll be coming back to Aachen. Sigrid has arranged for you to go for a week to her grandparents in Copenhagen . . . Your mum's fine . . . She'll call you later . . . The baby? When you come, you'll see it . . . No, Tina my teeny, don't call it 'Mr Michalis's baby', you'll just upset mum . . . Yes, your gran told me . . . No, I'm not going to tell you off, I just hope you didn't catch cold . . . But it was a mad thing to do . . . Look, just try and do what she tells you . . . Love you lots . . .

On Monday morning, I went off to school. I was looking forward to seeing Wick again, since our lives were so similar.

I took a small rucksack and left my school bag at home – it weighs a ton. We weren't going to have maths, but I didn't understand what we were going to have instead, because the kids had said that on Monday we'd be having 'Acidin'. I'd never heard of it, but I was too shy to ask. I thought it must be some kind of national memorial day.

When I arrived at school, I found a crowd gathered outside – mums and dads, and some police nearby. Hanging on the railings was a massive red banner with the word 'Sit-In' written in black letters. It's lucky I hadn't asked, as I'd obviously got it wrong – I'd just have looked ridiculous.

At the gate I saw several older kids telling everyone who had turned up: 'Quick, quick, get inside'. As soon as the last kid got in, one of the Third Years locked the door with a gigantic padlock hanging from a big chain.

I couldn't understand what was going on. The playground was full of kids, some talking, some shouting, others singing, and some writing on the walls of the school building.

I wandered round among them feeling lost, until I caught sight of Vicky and ran over to her.

– Did you bring any food? she asked. They're planning to keep us all locked in for the whole day, maybe even for the night as well.

I was terrified: I hated the thought of being locked in at school. Vicky explained that the sit-in committee had said that if our demands weren't met by the Ministry, we might even be stuck behind bars for several days. In one corner of the playground a group of children were chanting: 'We're the kids of the Hell-E-NIC NAY-SHUN – Where's the Mi-ni-ster of ED-YU-CAY-SHUN?!' Others were hanging off the railings, talking to their parents gathered outside. I went into the building with Vicky. Passing the staffroom we looked through the glass door and saw all the teachers and the headmistress, who was nervously fiddling with her haircombs and drinking one glass of water after another.

Mr Benos was sitting on top of a desk. Suddenly, he got up and came towards the door. Vicky and I thought he was going to come out and we'd be able to ask him what was happening, but then we heard the key turn twice in the lock and saw him go back to where he'd been sitting. Apparently he was just locking the door, not opening it. I don't know why, but that made me feel frightened.

Vicky pulled me away, and we began to roam around the empty classooms. In one of them there were several kids sitting on top of the desks; as soon as they saw us they started to shout:

– Go away, we're taking a vote. We'll tell you the result later.

We went back down to the playground.

– What a really great performance this sit-in committee has put on for us, said Vicky crossly.

Then I completely lost it. One thing I knew for sure: no way was I staying locked in there all day. I went over to the railings. Outside on the street, half hidden behind a tree, I saw Wick signalling to me, trying to tell me something.

I told Vicky I wasn't feeling well – actually my stomach did feel awful – and that I needed to go outside.

– It's true, you do look really pale, she said.

We pushed our way through the kids to get to the school gate, but their fingers seemed to be holding me back like a spider's web. I managed to open up a narrow passage, but the webs seemed to block it again, and I was tugging, tugging at them so I could get out, but then it was as if Vicky gathered them up into a ball, and we made it to the gate.

Vicky told the boy who was standing guard to open up so I could go home, because I wasn't well.

He replied that no one was allowed to leave, even if they were dying. I nearly passed out. Vicky grabbed the boy by his jacket. What she told him I can't repeat, but he wouldn't give way.

He was saying that they knew all about me, that I didn't care about anything that happened at the school, and I was only pretending to be foreign, as if I'd just landed from the moon, like that other kid – the one from Year Three, the German.

The spider's web was spinning itself around me, wrapping me up completely, and I couldn't see or hear anything. When I opened my eyes, there was a crowd of kids standing over me.

Vicky gave me some air by waving an exercise book in front of my face, until finally a girl from one of the senior classes came and undid the padlock. She opened the gate a narrow crack so I could get through.

One of the mums standing outside gave me a drink of orange juice from a carton she was holding. She asked me if I was going to be able to get home on my own. I told her I lived close by.

I walked away. In the square, beneath the statue of Admiral Kounaris, I found Wick waiting for me, feeding the pigeons with bread rolls.

– Let's get away from here, it's too close to my gran's house, I said.

We ran onto Fokionos Negri Street and began to walk down the long avenue. For a while we didn't speak at all.

– Seems to me you don't want to go home, said Wick.

I made a sign for 'No'. But I felt awful, only just about managing to keep on my feet. A bit further down we came to a café called *The Atrium.*

– Let's go in here, I suggested, but Wick pulled me away, saying it was too expensive.

– I'll treat you, I said, and though there were tables outside I went in, and Wick followed.

We sat at a small table in the middle, behind a tall pillar.

He ordered a coffee with milk and a lot of sugar, and I had a fruit juice.

Why did that boy say I don't care about anything and that I'm pretending to be foreign? I felt like having a good moan, even if I didn't know Wick all that well. Perhaps it was because he had the wolf with the hole hanging from his neck. But he wasn't any comfort at all.

– You think we aren't foreign? Our parents move us around like suitcases. They get a thing about Germany. Greece makes them see red. Even if you're mad about the piano – tough, that's the end of the piano, finito. Just practise on a computer keyboard, it's all the same. And they just 'rebuild their lives' whenever they want to.

I didn't like the way he talked about our parents.

– I love my mum and dad a lot, but the way things have turned out . . .

I couldn't finish, I just burst into tears.

Wick said that he'd been like that at the start, he used to snivel just like me. I was really offended that he called it 'snivelling', and I tried to stop. He paid no attention and just carried on, and said that he got tired of crying and found the solution. He took a little pill from his pocket, and swallowed it down quickly with a gulp of coffee. Then he put his hand back in his pocket and held out a sky-blue pill in the palm of his hand; just like the one the German had given me at Proussos.

– Take it and you'll feel better, he said. I always do, with the blue ones, the yellow, the white. Only thing is, they're expensive.

I said he should tell me what they're called, so I could buy some at the chemist and give him one back. He began to laugh:

– Are you from outer space? You really are just a kid, aren't you?

Then he told me, almost in a whisper, as if he didn't want to be overheard – though there was only one elderly man sitting in the café with his face buried in his newspaper, and the girl who'd served us had disappeared into a room behind the cash till . . .

– You can only get them on prescription. But if you've got forty euros, even twenty will do, you can buy some from Dr Vinegar Face.

Maybe I was from outer space, because I couldn't follow what he meant, and it was some time before he managed to make me understand that they'd come across (they? he and who else?) some doctor who gave them what they needed, as long as they paid him.

I swallowed the pill with my juice, and I started to feel better straight away, just like I did at Proussos.

I called the girl over and paid, while Wick, glancing at the bill, mumbled 'thanks' for his coffee.

– Didn't I tell you it was expensive here!

We left and started to make our way further down Fokionos Negri.

Feeling happy and light-hearted, I turned and looked at Wick. He seemed to be staring into space. Wait, what was the name of that boy in the third year at the grammar school in Aachen? He stopped coming to school and the other kids said he was 'taking substances'. Us kids in the First Year didn't understand what 'substances' were. Next day though, a lady doctor came into our class and gave us a talk about drugs.

'Wick, are you taking drugs?'

I think I said this to myself, but even if I said it out loud, he wasn't listening. I really wanted to ask him what was in those little blue pills. Whatever it was, I felt ab-so-lute-ly great, just like I did at Proussos.

Wick looked dead ahead, raised his hand as if he was the King of Fokionos Negri, and greeted everyone sitting at the café and restaurant tables as we passed by. Suddenly his eyes turned golden, shining like fairy lights.

– In Cologne, I started playing the piano when I was six. That's why they sent me to music school. They didn't need to tell me to practise, I used to play all day long. I didn't want to do anything else. I was really into the piano. I even won a prize. But my piano got left behind. 'You'll come back and carry on with your studies' – they lied to me, both of them. Why shouldn't I hate them? In my dreams, I often feel my fingers moving as if they were playing of their own accord. It doesn't bother me any more. I've got the pills, and something else that's even more amazing.

But before I could ask him anything else, he called 'bye', and left me standing on my own in the middle of the road.

So now, Tina, we'll go back to Kaloyerá – that's the little street where gran's house is – and you can just be like Wick, don't let anything bother you.

I press the doorbell, leaving my finger on the button.

Dinnnnng!

Nobody.

Farmor must have gone out, and as she thinks I'm still at school, she's not back yet. She keeps the spare key in the kitchen drawer. One day I'm just going to take it. I'll soon be thirteen, I've a right to my own key.

Dinnnnng!

I'll ring until she gets back.

There she is, I can just see her coming round the corner. She's pulling the shopping trolley along. I'm certainly not going to go and help her. She's quite close now . . .

Dinnnnng!

– Have you gone mad? You can see I'm coming.

Dinnnnng!

– Pity you didn't leave me a key. In Aachen I had one when I was eight.

Dinnnnng!

She leaves the trolley standing and prises my finger from the button.

– You'll disturb the neighbours.

– Who cares about the neighbours?

– Tina! What's wrong with you? she says, and unlocks the door.

She went inside, and I followed her, leaving the trolley outside on the pavement. She had to go back and fetch it in herself.

– Why have you finished school so early? Have you been sent home?

– The school had 'Acidin'!

She's giving me such a weird look that I start to laugh. I do her a favour and give her the correct version:

– A 'sit-in'.

I run to my room and close the door. I can't stop laughing. It seems to be upsetting Herr Heiner; he comes out of his nest covered in cotton wool, wearing it like a little cape. Standing to attention in front of his cage, I give him a bow.

– Dear Herr Heiner, I'm not the Tina you used to know, the one who snivels all the time, as Wick calls it. Now I'm a different Tina, much happier, and I don't care if my parents drag me around like a suitcase. They get a thing about Greece. Germany makes them see red. One of them wants Mr Michalis, the other one wants Frau Sabrina. They don't ask Tina what she wants. Let's wrap her up like a parcel and send her to Farmor by courier.

'But Tina's not bothered any more. Wick'll find

Vinegar Face and get a prescription for some miracle pills.

'If you only knew how fantastic I'm feeling. Now where am I going to get the money? Not to worry. Nope, I'm not going to steal from Farmor's purse, nor from Little Demi's, though in her case it'd be no problem – she's always forgetting it and ringing us when she gets back home to ask if we've found it . . .

'I'll take a few of those useless stamps that Farmor keeps in the drawer. Those Kurds have more than enough with all the stuff she keeps giving them. Anyway, what would the Kurds do with those stamps that Farmor inherited from her uncle? Smart Demi says each one is incredibly valuable. There are so many of them, she'll never notice. It's not as if she looks at them every day – in fact, she probably hardly ever looks at them at all.

'You can't call that stealing. Taking a stamp isn't theft; it's just what you might do to post a letter. You hardly recognise me, you say? But I like myself like this. Just wait and see – I'm going to make a whole new me!'

I start to laugh again. I go to the mirror, take hold of a bunch of hair on top of my head, and tie it tightly with an elastic band. Let's see what Farmor thinks of that!

Little Herr Heiner turns his back on me and burrows into his nest. He doesn't like the new Tina, it seems.

Farmor calls me for supper. I leave my room, go straight to the table, and start to eat immediately, without waiting for her. It's chicken with rice, my favourite.

– What's that top-knot thing on your head?

I had my head bent down to the plate, so I hadn't even noticed she'd sat down.

– You're the one who told me I shouldn't let my hair fall in my eyes.

– You could have used a hair clip. Your hair doesn't need to flop down like that.

– It's my hair, I'll do what I want with it!

– No need to shout, I'm not deaf! Are you going to your German class like that?

I hadn't realised I was shouting.

– What's my German class got to do with the elastic band?

– Tina, you're not a stupid child, you're actually very clever. But at times I despair of you.

'I despair of you, ALL the time.' I said that silently, deep down inside myself.

When I went to my room to get ready for the German lesson, I felt suddenly tired, and my legs were shaking. I just wanted to sleep. I let myself fall down on the bed.

I heard Farmor coming up and giving me a shake:

– Are you asleep? You'll be late.

I got up, but my head felt heavy. I took the German books and made as if to go.

– Do something about your hair, said Farmor.

She said it three times.

I didn't reply. I dashed to the front door and she

caught hold of me from behind.

– You don't seem to realise just how ridiculous you look . . .

I was already on the street, but I couldn't walk properly. This blue pill doesn't last long, does it? I thought the one at Proussos lasted much longer. In that case, I'm going to have to take them all the time, as they make me feel . . . ace. That's a new word I've learnt. I'll get hold of Wick tomorrow. But I'm not in the mood for German right now, and it's not because of the hair. What if I don't go to my lesson? Maybe I can find him on Fokionos Negri.

They say it starts with pills and ends with heroin. Well, that's what that lady doctor said when she came to our school in Aachen. She must have meant a different kind of pill though, because these blue ones make you feel really good. It's true I'm feeling rotten just now, but if I take them all the time . . .

I was walking along Fokionos Negri and I'd decided I definitely wasn't going to German. I sat down on a bench, then I saw him coming towards me from a long way off. Looking just like an angel, with his curly chestnut-blond hair and his dark blue eyes. Mr Benos!

As he came nearer, I tried to take the elastic band off my hair. But I'd tied it so tight that I couldn't undo it. I gave up and let my hand drop onto the back of the bench.

– Hello there, Tina. Been taking a stroll?

– Hello, Mr Benos. I have a German lesson. Just . . . on my way there now.

But suddenly I felt I couldn't lie to Mr Benos, any more than I could to Herr Heiner. He came and sat down next to me on the bench.

– You know, I don't think I'm going to go to the lesson.

– Tina, you truant! he said laughing.

I told him I didn't feel well. I didn't mention the pill I'd taken.

– I didn't want to stay at home. I live with my gran and we're always fighting like cat and dog.

As I was talking, he was looking at me with blue eyes that seemed full of love.

And then the old Tina suddenly appeared – the one who sat in the *Café Roncalli* pouring out her heart and soul to Herr Heiner while sipping her hot chocolate, and I told myself that if I talked to Mr Benos, I could keep that other Tina close by – sometimes I thought she'd vanished for ever.

I told him my whole life story. I even explained why I call gran 'Farmor'. I told him about the Aachen Tina, out with her dad in the Annastrasse in the evenings, and going ice-skating on Sundays. I told him about mum, what a fantastic teacher she is and how much the kids love her, about Sigrid and Leonardo di Caprio, my little hamster, and of course about Herr Heiner. And finally I told him about the day when everything had turned upside down.

I stopped and turned to look at him, because I'd told him all that looking into the distance, rather like Venetia. I thought he was staring at my top-knot, and I tried to tug at it.

– Leave your hair alone, and listen to me.

– Farmor says I can't go to German with my hair like this.

He laughed.

– I don't think it's that that's stopping you, my dear Tina.

It had been so long since anyone called me 'dear'. I felt my head starting to feel heavy again. Mr Benos was worried I might be unwell, and told me to go home. I found the energy to shout:

– No! . . . No!

He was trying to calm me down, to find out what was wrong with me.

Because apart from what I'd told him, he said, there must be something wrong with my health. Tomorrow we'd have a chat during break, because I was perplexing him; but now I really ought to go home. I was glad that I was perplexing him, even if I didn't know exactly what it meant.

He held my freezing cold hands in his, just like when dad and I found a bird lying in the Annastrasse, numb with cold, and dad picked it up and put his hands around it to warm it back to life.

OK, I didn't snivel, but some tears did run down my cheeks.

I want my dad. I want my mum. I want my feather duvet.

I heard Mr Benos's voice as if coming from a long way away.

He was saying that there were a whole lot of kids at the school who had divorced parents, and they weren't so lucky that their mums and dads were on such good terms as mine were. Yet somehow, they managed to get through it. Of course he could understand that my parents were a long way away, and that made things more difficult. But as I was only here for one year, I shouldn't despair . . . It'd pass quickly . . .

I didn't get the chance to tell him that actually it was going very, very slowly, because suddenly I noticed the three Demis approaching, and they were almost upon us.

I started to shake.

Mr Benos was totally unphased. They saw us straight away.

– Tina! they said in chorus.

Mr Benos stood up and introduced himself. Smart Demi's eyes lit up.

– I'm so pleased we've met you, Mr Benos, your fame has spread far and wide. I've heard from quite a few parents what a good teacher you are, and what a wonderful human being.

– That's too much, he laughed. It's just that I love my work and the kids.

Then he looked at me and continued:

– I met Tina on Fokionos Negri. She's one of my favourite pupils, but she wasn't feeling at all well and we sat down here for a bit so she could recover. I was planning to accompany her home.

Little Demi jumped in and interrupted him:

– Many many thanks, because we – I'm sorry, we haven't introduced ourselves, she said, and began to reel off their names – We're friends of her grandmother, I say friends, but more like sisters really, and so Tina is our granddaughter, and . . .

Smart Demi interrupted the flow, we said goodbye to Mr Benos, and the three Demis took me home.

– What a handsome young man, said Little Demi.

– He's a wonderful human being, that's what counts, said Smart Demi.

– Well, whatever he is, he's certainly not doing any harm, said Big Demi, who until then hadn't said anything at all.

I could scarcely manage to drag my feet. Farmor looked shocked when we finally showed up. Before she could even get a word out, the others explained everything. She turned and looked at me with that fixed glare.

– All very well, but what were you doing on Fokionos Negri Street?

She asked three times, but didn't get a reply. Then her voice softened, it became almost gentle. She came up close and laid the palm of her hand on my forehead.

– You don't have a fever. But you're very pale, go and lie down.

That was exactly what I needed. I rushed to my room, collapsed on the bed, and all I wanted to do was sleep.

– If the stamps turn out to be really valuable, I'll buy Wick a piano, I murmured, just as I fell into a deep slumber.

CHAPTER SIX

When I woke up, it was broad daylight outside. I didn't feel very happy, but I didn't feel tired either. It was as if nothing could get to me, as if my mind was a complete blank.

Farmor opened the door very quietly. A sweet old granny, like the ones in the fairy tales.

– I phoned the doctor yesterday – he told me to let you sleep as much as you want to. Do you want to get up? Shall I make you some breakfast? It's a bit early for school.

She didn't need to say it three times – I told her I'd had enough sleep. I got up, went up to the mirror, and the first thing I did was to take an even bigger bunch of hair and bind it tightly on the top of my head with an elastic band. I don't know why, but with that top-knot that Farmor hated so much, I felt more sure of myself.

As soon as I went into the kitchen for breakfast, I saw her glaring at my hair. But she didn't say anything. It was only when I'd picked up my bag and was going off to school that she had a go:

– Your wonderful Mr Benos, hasn't he said

anything to you about your hairstyle?

– Mr Benos doesn't mind what hairstyles we have. It's enough if we know our lessons. One kid in our class has his hair in dreadlocks, but Mr Benos doesn't say anything about it, because he's top of the class.

– What on earth are dreadlocks? . . .

– I'll do my hair like that tomorrow, so you can see, I interrupted her.

– Well if you're in a mood to argue about hairstyles, at least that means you're feeling better. But I don't want to see that top-knot again, I mean it seriously.

– You won't see it again. I said it just like a good little girl, and went out onto the street.

I was very, very angry. The main thing that mum and dad care about is that I'm OK, not whether I'm wearing a hair-slide or an elastic band.

Within seconds, I'd made up my mind. She wouldn't see the top-knot again. But I had to get Wick to give me a blue pill, otherwise I couldn't get up the nerve to do what had occurred to me, in a flash, as I was leaving the house.

At school no one was in a mood to learn, neither the kids nor the teachers. The headmistress had changed her hair combs and was wearing a blue one with shiny stones. She went from class to class to see if there were any teachers absent.

We didn't have a lesson with Mr Benos. But he tracked me down at break and asked me if I was feeling OK. He could tell my mind was on other things.

While he was speaking to me, I was looking round for Wick – maybe he was playing truant again.

Mr Benos asked me to get Farmor's permission, because he wanted to take the class to the theatre on Saturday. Some great play or other about kids of my age.

I told him I'd ask, and he went back to the staff room, where he said they were having a discussion about the sit-in.

Vicky rushed up to me.

– Teacher's pet!

– Whose?

– Benos, don't pretend you don't know.

– Whatever, I said, and left her standing there, as I carried on looking for Wick.

He'd vanished into thin air.

I found him when school was over, near Kaloyerá, dragging his feet along the pavement . . .

I headed away from our street, so as not to bump into Farmor or one of the Demetrias, and he followed me.

– Don't rush, he said breathlessly, as we reached Fokionos Negri and he slumped onto a bench.

– What's wrong with you? I asked anxiously.

– I ate a hot dog and it's given me food poisoning, he laughed, but rather strangely.

I took twenty euros out of my pocket, that I'd been saving to buy the new CD that they'd told me they'd have in next week at the shop.

He gave me a blue pill. It was his last one. He'd take the money to Vinegar Face to get a new prescription.

I gulped it down with a bottle of water I had in my school bag. I told him I wanted to cut off all my hair.

He wasn't at all phased. He had a friend who was a hairdresser, 'a bit of a fairy, but he'll cut your hair any way you want. His shop is a few streets away.'

We took the bus, because he couldn't face walking. That hot dog must have been really off.

The hairdresser had dyed blond hair and a high-pitched voice like a girl's. I was starting to feel happy again, no worries at all. I told him to shave my head because I had nits, and I was allergic to the medical shampoos. I was getting really good at lying.

Wick wasn't really listening, he just called 'See you', and left the shop, stumbling over the doorstep.

I sat down in the chair, and Riccardo – that was the hairdresser's name – put a white towel around my neck. I closed my eyes and listened to the whirring of the shaver.

– The schools are full of headlice, I heard Riccardo saying. The other day they brought three boys here – I shaved them all as bald as a coot.

I didn't say anything.

– Don't worry, he consoled me. It's very fashionable right now. Yesterday a girl was in here, out and out punk, know what I mean? Seven holes in each ear, rings on her eyebrows. By the time I'd finished she looked like a harvest moon.

He removed the towel and I felt the brush sweeping the hairs off the nape of my neck.

– That's it.

I opened my eyes. In the mirror I saw an alien from outer space. With protruding ears and enormous dark eyes. I wanted to burst out laughing, but I held it in.

– It'll grow back quickly. You've got healthy hair.

Of course, Riccardo thought I needed sympathy. I paid and left in a hurry. I took the bus, so as not to be even later. Nobody noticed. I glanced at myself in the windows and thought my headphones would go well with the haircut. I took them out of the bag and put them on. Good old Silver Moon helped me to have the nerve to go through with it.

I pressed the bell, not too much, just two short rings.

It was Farmor who opened the door, of course. She looked at me for a moment as if she didn't know who I was, then turned deathly pale and rushed back into the house.

I went in. I took off my headphones.

– Well I promised you wouldn't see the top-knot any more, I said in a cheerful idiot kind of way.

Farmor didn't even look at me. She got up with difficulty from the armchair she'd collapsed into, went to the phone and dialled the Demetrias one after the other, just like the time she told me about, when she wanted to tell them her plan for getting grandad out of the clutches of the Germans.

I ran to my room, where I burst into a really loud laughing fit. Herr Heiner poked his little snout out of his nest, to see what was up. I opened the cage, stuck my hand inside, and stroked him with my finger between his eyes, the way he likes.

Now I am absolutely and totally the other Tina. I think I'm getting used to it. I'm not sorry for anything. I couldn't care less if Mr Michalis's baby says 'mummy' to my mum, or if I have to have Brigitte as a sister.

Why don't they give out those sky-blue pills at the chemist's without a prescription? We ought to keep a store of them at school like vitamin pills. They just don't want the kids to be happy, that's all it is!

Diiiiing Diiiiing!

I wonder which of the Demetrias has got here first? I bet all of them together, Little Demi will have picked them up in her old banger.

I can hear their voices, and Farmor's voice too, no longer subdued, but loud and clear as a bell. I open the door of my room to listen.

– She doesn't obey anyone at all. It's a disgrace!

– Well, my little rebel soldier girl, in that case she's just like you! chuckled Little Demi.

– It's no time for jokes, said Smart Demi sternly.

– I had beliefs, said Farmor.

I heard the voice of Big Demi as well, but as she spoke softly, I couldn't make out what she was saying. I rushed in with my head down, as if I was diving into the ocean.

– Hello there.

Sometimes when I get back from my German classes and Farmor is in the kitchen preparing something, I lounge about in front of the television and zap around on the remote. If I chance on some soap or other, and see one of the actors with eyes wide, or some actress frozen with her mouth open, I realise that's the end of the episode and the credits will be rolling any moment.

Well, that's exactly how it was: The Demetrias all standing there as if they'd been turned to stone. Little Demi had her mouth wide open, Smart Demi had her eyebrows knitted together, and Big Demi had shed a tear that stayed hanging out of the corner of her eye.

But the credits didn't roll, and the episode wasn't over yet. Smart Demi said that after the war they used to cut off the hair of girls who'd gone with German soldiers, so everyone could point at them and spit on them.

– Never mind all that now, Little Demi interrupted her.

Farmor said my dad would be really upset if he could see the state I'm in.

I was still feeling brave from the pill, and I said that I bet my dad would like it. In Aachen, at my old school, quite a few of the girls had the same haircut, and nobody said a thing. One Sunday I even saw a girl come out of church with a totally bald head . . .

– Actually, the other day I saw a girl on the street near here with large gold earrings and a shaved head, said Big Demi, quietly.

– Don't tell me it's the fashion, and we've just slept through it? said Little Demi, laughing. But fashion or no fashion, young lady, you look a right mess, and I hope your hair grows back quickly.

The awful thing was, I was beginning to feel sick – it seemed that the more you took, the shorter the pills lasted. And I was wondering if I'd get through the evening at German class, and the following day at school.

Farmor got the Demis to stay and have dinner with us. I guess she didn't want to stay on her own with me. I felt the same way, even if Smart Demi kept looking at me like some disgusting insect.

I gulped down my food at lightning speed, then got up to go to my room and get ready for German class. Before I closed the door, I could hear them talking.

– Whatever you say, Ismeni, I'm convinced something's happened to that child recently, said Little Demi.

– Like what for instance? She's just got a rebellious nature, that's all, said Farmor.

I shut the door so as not to hear any more. I lay down on my bed, as I wasn't feeling all that brilliant. Wick had said that if I could get him a large amount of money, he could get Vinegar Face to give him a more powerful prescription. There's a pill that you put underneath your tongue, and as soon as it dissolves, you're totally sorted. I didn't understand what 'totally sorted' meant, but I wasn't going to ask him that until he brought it along. I just needed to be left alone in the house for a minute, to dig out the stamps.

Someone knocked at the door of my room.

Couldn't be Farmor, she wasn't one for knocking.

I sat up quickly, said 'Come in', and Little Demi appeared.

I managed to smile at her, and she sat down next to me and stroked my head. I must have pulled away suddenly, because she said quickly:

– It's OK, I'm not going to ask any questions . . . Some other time. I just wanted to tell you we're going out on a jaunt up to Kaisariani, to have a coffee. She could do with a bit of fresh air. When you go out to German, shut the door properly.

– She doesn't give me a key, I can't lock it.

– Doesn't matter if it's left unlocked for a couple of hours, just give it a good pull to close it tight.

She kissed me on the top of my head, and went out. I didn't dare believe it. Two hours on my own at home. Of course it'd mean skiving off my German class again.

A short while later I heard the front door close. Farmor didn't bother to say 'Goodbye'.

I went into her room and ran straight to the chest of drawers. Once, when she'd shown the Demis her stamps, she'd left her door open and I'd seen her take a big dark green album out of the chest of drawers.

I opened the drawer. It was full of photographs, filled right to the top. Men and women, all of them in military uniform.

As I was lifting them up carefully so as not to mix them up, I noticed a large photo. It was a young girl, with a beret on; her curly black hair hung down to her shoulders, and it was as if she was looking me right in the eye. She was wearing a soldier's jacket, with large pockets over the breast, and she was holding a rifle, with her finger on the trigger. Her lips were set together, but her face was gentle, and her eyes seemed to radiate a brilliant light.

It was Farmor! She looked so young, and so saintly, even though she had a gun in her hand. She looked as if she was ready to shoot, believe me. She'd obviously posed for the photograph. Her trigger finger was long and slender. Without wanting to, without even understanding why, I picked up the photo and kissed the girl on the eyes. She looked just like dad. Maybe like me too?

I carried on searching, and right down at the bottom of the drawer I discovered the album I was looking for. I sat down on Farmor's bed and began to turn the pages. The stamps were wrapped in cigarette paper, each one separately. I guessed that the oldest ones, and certainly the ones that there was only a single copy of, would be the most valuable, because lots of them had two or three copies. I took three from different pages, so it wouldn't be obvious that they were missing. Then I put the album carefully back under the photos, and pulled the bedspread straight, so you couldn't tell anyone had sat on it. It was only when I got into my room that my heart stopped beating wildly. I put the stamps in an envelope, grabbed my school bag and went out to look for Wick, pulling the door shut as I left.

It didn't take long to find him. I went to the bar he hangs out at. He was drinking a juice, and seemed in a far better state than he'd been in when I last saw him.

– You've recovered from the hot dog? I asked.

– What hot dog? he said, as if it was news to him . . .

I changed the subject.

– I've brought some stamps.

He jumped up, and his eyes turned golden again. I gave him the envelope, he glanced inside and stuffed it into his pocket.

I've no idea about all that stuff, he muttered, and then asked me: What are you doing now?

– Skiving off German.

– Great. I'll take you to meet Lady Di. She knows about everything.

I didn't ask him anything else, not even who this 'Lady' is. He just told me, she's a painter and lives nearby.

A few streets down, we stopped in front of the main door of a new block of flats. Before we got into the lift, Wick gave me a serious look.

– Swear that you'll never come here on your own.

I swore. Why not? – it didn't seem any big deal.

We went up to the sixth floor – to the penthouse, as Wick called it. He didn't ring the bell, he just rapped out a rhythm on the door.

The door was opened by a girl who looked exactly like Diana, the Princess of Wales, in her super-thin phase. Deep blue eyes, but with large dark circles round them, and a hairstyle the spitting image of Lady Di's. She was wearing a tight-fitting black skirt, and her bones were showing so much, I was wondering if she had any flesh at all on her body.

– Hi, she said to Wick, then took a good look at me, cowering behind him. Who's this creature from Mars you've dragged in?

– Wait till you see what she's brought us!

– Is that so? she said, and stepped aside to let us in.

– Not what you're thinking, but it's something really great, said Wick, and pulled out the envelope.

She took it, opened it, took out the stamps, went to a big table laden with paints and brushes, ferreted out a magnifying glass and began to study them.

I was standing in the middle of the room looking round at the pictures, some hanging on the walls; others stood on the floor, apparently only half-finished.

In Aachen, I often went to the art galleries, and at home we had books on painting that I used to leaf through with dad. But I'd never seen paintings as horrible as these before. Faces with holes for eyes and women's bodies without heads. One woman with her legs open and a sword thrust between them, and another with a naked breast and a nipple cut off, from which blood was flowing.

I closed my eyes so as not to see any more. I could hear Lady Di's voice, talking to Wick.

– Where did she get them?

– From her grandmother's.

– Are there any more?

– A whole album full, I heard myself saying loudly.

– Tomorrow I'll take them to this place I know, so they can have a look at them. I'll let you know, she said to Wick, as if I wasn't there and the stamps belonged to him.

– You don't have anything for this evening? Wick was almost begging.

– Nix, zilch, I'm telling you . . . Come round later on . . . Maybe then. Does your friend from Mars need some as well?

– I'll come on my own, said Wick, and I couldn't understand why he dragged me away by the hand so forcibly, to get me to leave with him.

As soon as we got into the lift, he repeated:

– Promise me you'll never come here to see Lady Di on your own.

I was lying down on my bed, and doing what Wick had told me to do when I needed a pill. 'Hasn't your granny got any sleeping pills, any painkillers? . . . ' 'My gran doesn't take medicine. In the bathroom cupboard there's only aspirin and a cough syrup they send me from Germany.' 'From Germany? Great. Because the ones they sell here don't do anything at all. Get it down you as fast as you can.'

I drank quite a bit of it. It made me feel a bit dizzy, and then that young girl with the gun in her hands appeared. It was a struggle not to go to sleep. Farmor had to find me awake. I wasn't worried any more about going to school with my head looking the way it did. I'd tell them I had nits, and about my allergy. All of them. Yes, all of them, even Mr Benos. But I felt bad about it. No, I couldn't lie to Mr Benos like that.

Farmor came into the room and stood opposite me, looking at me, holding her rifle, her finger on the trigger. But she wasn't posing for a photograph, she was ready to attack me. I was thrashing around, trying to get free of the spiders' web coiling all round me, I tried to shout 'No' but the the web got into my mouth.

– Nooooo!

– What are you shouting for? Did you fall asleep? When are you going to do your homework?

Standing next to my bed was Farmor. Not the girl in the photo. The Farmor with the angry eyebrows. I sat up in bed and looked at her with a blank expression.

– How did the German class go? she asked.

– What German class?

– Are you asleep? she said, and gave me a shake.

I got up. I fetched my bag.

Farmor left the room.

The phone rang, she answered.

– Yes . . . she was asleep . . . she spends half the night listening to tapes and it makes her tired next day . . . No, she's not coughing . . . yes, the syrup you sent her.

– I snatched the receiver from her hand. She didn't say anything. I could hear my own breathing.

– Tina my teeny, the doctor says, if I take care, in a short while I'll be dancing again . . . No, silly, I won't have a limp, but it seems to have been a difficult fracture . . . Yes, as soon as I can walk properly . . .

– Can't you come now . . . even if you're still limping?

– Be patient, sweetheart . . . as soon as I can walk, I'll be there.

– Now, dad, please . . . come now!

Farmor took the receiver away from me.

– Come on, this is costing enough already. Sure, we're fine here.

Next morning, before I went to school, for dutch courage I decided to drink the rest of the cough syrup, but I was afraid it might not make any difference, and it could be days before they sent me some more.

At school you'd think they were going to put up a statue in my honour. They completely forgot about the sit-in: everyone was obsessed with my head. Nits and an allergy.

Greek Geek cried, and lots of kids put dots on my shaven head with their pens. Even the headmistress believed me when she asked me into her office for a chat.

Mr Benos gave me a searching look:

– At the end of school, don't go, wait for me.

Vicky was sure I'd done it as a fashion statement. She'd seen a Hollywood actress with a shaven head in a magazine.

– But what a body she had! Whereas you look like a bald grasshopper . . .

I didn't wait for Mr Benos. As soon as the bell went I left straight away, because I knew Wick would be waiting for me down the road, and I'd find out what had happened with the stamps.

He didn't have to tell me, I could see straight away, because he was grinning from ear to ear. They were worth a lot, he said, and he gave me a slip of paper on which Lady Di's expert had written down some other stamps I should try to find. Wick thought it would be easy for me to get into Farmor's room. He'd go and see Vinegar Face that evening, he said, and get a whole wodge of prescriptions.

– I'll see you at five at *The Atrium*.

– But it's expensive – you said so yourself.

– We've got money.

– I'll be at my German class.

– To hell with your German – I'll be expecting you! he called to me as I was leaving.

I arrived home puffing and panting. I was wondering if I should say 'to hell' with my German, but then maybe Wick would bring me a lovely pill later and I'd be up for it.

You'd think Farmor had deliberately gone and cooked lentils, because she knows I hate them. They're full of iron, she says, and I should eat them.

We sat at the table. Facing one another, not talking at all.

– What did they say at school about your hair?

What did they say at school about your hair? Well, what did they say? At school? About your hair?

Three times she'd said it, so I had to reply.

– That I look like a Hollywood actress.

She let her spoonful of lentils fall back on the plate without putting it to her mouth. She was going to say something, but she saw me get up, and so I guess she thought better of it.

– Where are you going?

– To my German class.

– What, so early?

– Some of the other kids are expecting me so we can talk about a study project we have to do together.

– At least take a satsuma in your bag with you.

I grabbed an orange and ran to my room. Or rather it was the other Tina who ran in there, Tina the Liar. Herr Heiner didn't even budge from inside his nest, even though I tapped on the bars of his cage. It's as if he doesn't want to lay eyes on me. And as for me . . . to hell with it, as Wick would say. If I can only get a pill, I'll tell Farmor exactly where she gets off, and if Herr Heiner makes faces at me, I'll give him what for!

No, not the other Herr Heiner – probably best not to think about him.

CHAPTER SEVEN

The Atrium was nearly empty. Except for one table where two men were sitting: white hair, dark suits and ties. They were drinking ouzo and doing crossword puzzles. Wick was nowhere to be seen.

I sat down and ordered a hot chocolate. As soon as the waitress brought it, steaming hot, I felt my stomach turning over. Why had I ordered it? I must have been mad. Just to bring back memories of *King's College* and the *Café Roncalli* and my dad and Herr Heiner? Come on then, Wick. Bring us the pills!

I'd just finished wishing when someone came in who looked like Wick's twin brother, but it definitely wasn't him. His hair was washed, bright and honey-coloured. He was wearing dark blue velvet trousers, a black jacket, and underneath a very clean white shirt. If he hadn't been so thin, I'd have said he was handsome.

It was Wick!

I was riveted to my seat. He came and sat next to me.

– Do I look presentable? Because I'm going to take you to a shop where they sell pianos.

Had he really got such a good price for the stamps? And how had he guessed I wanted to buy him a piano?!

– You're going to buy a piano? I gasped.

– No, idiot child, I'm going to play the piano. At the shop where they sell them they let you try them out, if you say you're thinking of buying one. Vinegar Face did me proud and I'm on top form, my fingers are itching, and I've absolutely got to play the piano.

Before I managed to ask him anything else, he took a pill out of his pocket and told me to put it underneath my tongue, then he paid for my chocolate and we left. We walked to Patission Avenue, then we took a bus.

I'd never seen Wick so happy.

– Don't I look like someone whose parents want to buy him a piano?

He did too. And as I sucked on the pill, my head slowly emptied, and all my cares disappeared – I even forgot about Herr Heiner the hamster, as well as the real Herr Heiner. I was really enjoying hanging out with Wick, with his honey-coloured hair.

We got out at Akadimias Street, in the centre of town. I tagged along behind him, wherever he was going. We reached Navarinou Street and the smart boutiques of Kolonaki, and I followed him into a shop selling pianos. An assistant asked Wick what he wanted.

– To try out the pianos.

– Up on the first floor, sir.

We went up. Wick looked utterly spellbound. There were grand pianos, uprights, lots and lots of different pianos. Two assistants came over, and Wick said he wanted to try out some of the instruments.

– Certainly, they said, just as you wish.

Wick sat down on a stool, opened the piano lid, pulled off the length of black cloth covering the keyboard, and started to play. His fingers flew over the keys, and I realised that it was Mozart.

Dad used to listen to a CD with that piece on practically every evening. As soon as we came back from our stroll in the Annastrasse, he'd sit down on the sofa, light a cigarette, and say: "Tina, my teeny, go and grab my Mozart!' I'd bring him the CD, sit next to him, lean my head on his shoulder, and we'd listen until mum came home from her course at the university.

But the memory didn't make me cry, because I felt so happy, as long as I carried on sucking the magic pill.

Wick was playing, and the assistants were standing listening to him. One of them went up to him.

– You're really good – and I can tell you I've heard a lot of them. Try some other models, if you'd like to.

Wick went from piano to piano, and as he played his long hair was shimmering like the waves of the sea. When he got up, his eyes were shining.

– I'll think it over and come to a decision, he said. I'll discuss it with my parents, then I'll be back.

– Whenever you want to, said one of the assistants, and they almost bowed.

Then, as we were going down the staircase, I noticed the curious looks they were giving me, the strange creature the great artist was dragging in his wake.

We went out onto the street. I wanted to talk to him, and was struggling to find the right words.

– You know . . . you play like . . . like Richter. I'd listened to a CD of his, with Dad.

Wick burst out laughing. I think it was only the second time I'd heard him laugh.

– I should certainly have you in my audience. Richter, eh?

I walked beside him and wished that something magic would happen and my hair would grow, even just a few centimetres would do. His bright honey hair rippled gently whenever he moved his head. He was fantastic. Why couldn't he always be like this?

– Let's do this again – we'll come to Navarinou, the two of us, so you can play the piano, and to hell with my German class.

– That's not going to happen, he replied in a small voice, which became sadder as he went on. I've just had a letter from the director of my music school in Cologne . . . he's still expecting me to go back . . . He says, whenever I want to I can go and live at his place, as long as I carry on studying the piano.

And then he fell silent. He led the way back to the bus. We got off one stop before Kypseli Square.

– We'll go by Lady Di's, he said, and I followed him.

I still felt happy. In my head, I could still see his fingers flying over the keys.

Lady Di opened the door. She was sucking on a long pipe, and seemed to be staggering. Her flat was full of people and full of smoke. The smell made me feel faint. Some people were sitting on the floor, others on the sofas, and they were all smoking.

– There's plenty on the table, said Lady Di to Wick.

He went to the table, took tobacco and cigarette papers from a jar, and began to roll a cigarette, and then a second one which he gave to me. I must have taken a step back, because he said:

– Don't be afraid, it's nothing bad – it's going to be legal here soon.

But I absolutely wouldn't. I've never smoked in my life. Herr Heiner was totally against cigarettes and he'd asked me to give him my word that I'd never smoke, and I'd given it. I'd given my word about other things and hadn't kept it. But this was one promise I was going to keep.

Wick was inhaling deeply and closing his eyes.

– You're weird. You swallow the pills down like sweets, and yet you won't touch this harmless stuff, which would help you chill out.

I didn't want to tell him about Herr Heiner, but even if I had done, he wasn't interested. He'd sat down on the floor and was smoking away. His face had taken on a strange expression, and he didn't look at all like the Wick who played the piano.

I opened the door and left. No one paid any attention to me. I took the lift and was still feeling great, as if I had an inner strength. Just what I needed to feed Farmor a load of lies.

As soon as I'd got to the ground floor, I renewed my solemn vow:

– No, Herr Heiner, I won't smoke any cigarettes, nor any of that stuff that makes Lady Di's place smell like a church.

Even when I was little, I couldn't bear the smell of incense. When we went to the Greek Orthodox church on feast days, as soon as my dad saw me turn pale, he'd take me out into the courtyard.

I skipped along to Kaloyerá Street.

Big Demi opened the door. Farmor and the others had gone to visit the Kurds, presumably to give them the blue and pink towelling robes.

Big Demi brought me a glass of milk – not from the fridge, natch – and a croissant, and she excused herself, as she had work in the kitchen. She'd promised Farmor to make a moussaka because the others would probably be late getting back.

– I'll just close the kitchen door while I'm frying the mince, she said.

I didn't drink my milk, or eat my croissant, I just ran to Farmor's room. I dug out the stamps again, took out the slip of paper Wick had given me, and since they were all carefully arranged in order in the album, I quickly picked out nine stamps.

When I went into the hall and heard the hissing of the meat frying, I took a deep breath.

But as soon as I got to my room I was sweating, and I collapsed in a heap as if all my strength had been drained out through the soles of my feet. And Wick had said that pill was really powerful. Big deal! It had certainly lasted longer than the other pills, the blue ones, but I still felt terrible again.

I went to lie down on the bed and then I saw Sigrid's letter, a white envelope lying on the grey blanket. I recognised her writing immediately – rounded letters with little tails on. I opened it straight away.

Dear Tinopoula – that was a pretend-Greek name she'd invented for me as a joke . . .

I don't understand . . . Your letter makes no sense at all. You tell me you don't want them to send you your computer, because Herr Heiner your hamster doesn't want it. Tinopoula, have you gone right round the bend? If you had your computer, you could get e-mail, and we could send one another messages every evening, just as we did in Aachen, and it would be as if you'd never left here.

How can Sigrid possibly understand – in order to fit the computer on the little orange table, first of all I'd have to throw out Herr Heiner.

I miss you a lot. You know who I'm hanging out with now? With Diagora. We're like chocolate and whipped cream, him being as black as night, and me extremely blonde. Last Sunday Brigitte invited me to your house. She's doing everything she can to become my best friend.

I couldn't read any more, because my eyes had filled with tears. Just think, Brigitte invited her to *my* house. What do you mean, your house, Tina? Your house is here now, in Kaloyerá, and your bed is that narrow little bunk with the grey blankets, and it's Brigitte who's now sleeping in your bed with the feather duvet and the mosquito net canopy, Brigitte, whose mum married your dad.

So I went, more in your memory than for any other reason. Straight away they took me to your room. My heart skipped a beat. No, it's not your room any more. And your bed isn't there. There's a single bed for Brigitte, a babyish quilt with a Snow White motif on it. None of your posters with the black horse and the frog are on the wall, your desk has gone, so has your chair, and your boots weren't there either, lying all over the floor. You can't imagine how glad I was to get out of there. I didn't see your father, he was away. Brigitte's mum was there. You know, she's really quite nice, we always said so, she's not at all like her daughter, and she's even prettier than before.

My heart stopped racing. Thanks dad, for not letting Brigitte sleep in my bed, or touch my things. But she can touch you. Do you go and give her a kiss before she goes to sleep every night? No, please don't . . .

I'll close for now, so I can start on my homework. Missing you lots.

With love and kisses,
Your best friend
Sigrid

P.S. Many greetings from Lord Sandwich. Yesterday there was another school trip to the town hall to see an exhibition.

I had to laugh, in spite of feeling so awful. They'd taken us to see the Town Hall in Aachen when we were in the fourth year at primary school. They told us its history, and then we noticed a portrait with a name underneath: 'LORD SANDWICH.' Our teacher noticed us sniggering at the name, and she told us his story.

It was true, that was his name. He was a nobleman who often went hunting and always took with him two pieces of bread, with cheese or meat between them. 'And so he invented the sandwich', we said and started to giggle.

I told Farmor and her friends that one day, just to say something amusing, because I was in the doghouse for something I'd done wrong. Why did I bother? They were outraged. 'So his name goes down in history for inventing the sandwich!' 'And here people have given their lives to save their country and they've been forgotten for ever.'

Why hadn't Wick given me any more pills? Why was he keeping them all for himself? Because he knows that I don't want to remember Aachen, that I just want to be the other Tina, the liar, the thief . . .

I heard Farmor and the Demis come back, and I pushed the letter underneath my pillow. I opened the door, before Farmor came and opened it herself. A swift noisy rattle of the handle, and next moment the door's wide open. That gets on my nerves more than anything else.

The smell of meat cooking came into my room, and I usually absolutely love it, but now it just made me feel sick . . . I went into the living room.

– What's wrong with you now? asked Farmor. You're very pale.

– I'm always pale.

– Not like now. Demetria, don't you think she's looking very pale?

– When she came back from her class she seemed fine, said Big Demi.

– How did your German go? asked Farmor.

– Great, the lying Tina managed to reply after the third time of asking.

We'd just sat down at the table, and when they put the plate of moussaka in front of me, I couldn't hold back, I ran to the bathroom and started to throw up. I could hear footsteps approaching.

– Can't I even puke on my own in this house!

This time I'd said it out loud .

– Tina!

– Tina!

– Konstantina!

I raised my head from the toilet bowl, with my face all smeared, and I saw all four of them crammed in the doorway of the bathroom. I must have looked a fright with my shaven head and the streaks of vomit around my mouth, because I saw four pairs of eyes fixed on me in amazement.

– What sort of language is that, my girl? said Smart Demi.

So that was what was bothering them. My 'language'. 'It makes me want to puke!' That's what I've heard Vicky say whenever she doesn't like something.

– Wipe your mouth clean, said Farmor and went to the medicine cupboard to look for something while I was cleaning myself up.

– Oh, when did you get through the whole bottle?

I looked up, with water still dripping down my face. In one hand she was holding a box of aspirin and in the other, the empty cough mixture bottle. I picked up the towel, and as I was drying myself I said:

– I was looking for an aspirin and I spilt it by accident.

– Careless as ever. I was wondering what made you so ill?

– I ate a cheese pastry in the canteen.

Another lie. How easy it was to fob them off!

– I've told you not to eat such rubbish, to take something with you from home. But do you listen? Now go and lie down, and when you've recovered, come and eat something.

Oh, the relief to be able to lie down. Mind, just hearing the word 'eat' made my stomach heave. I was fine while I was sucking that pill, and for ages afterwards – what was wrong with me now?

– Leave your door open so we can keep an eye on you, I heard Farmor say as I tottered across the room and collapsed on the bed.

– Whatever you say, Ismeni, I'm convinced something's happened to that child. She wasn't like that at the start.

Little Demi's soft voice, just about reaching my ears.

– Sh! Speak more quietly, said Farmor.

I'd closed my eyes and I was falling . . . falling . . .

Next morning I went to school with my feet dragging every step of the way. Just round the last corner before I got to school, Wick was waiting for me. Not the Wick I'd seen yesterday. You'd think he'd been through the washing machine, and had come out all creased and crumpled. His hair was still clean, but he'd scraped it back and tied it with an elastic band. It made his face look even thinner, and his eyes had shadows that were so dark, they looked as if they'd been painted on. He just about managed a 'hello', and gave me a pill.

– Under your tongue, he whispered.

– The other one didn't last long, I dared to protest.

– I don't make them, he replied cheekily, and turned to go.

– Wick . . .

I thought better of what I was going to say. But my voice stopped him in his tracks.

– Look, I said, taking out of my bag the piece of paper in which I'd folded the stamps.

– You went back to her house? he asked aggressively, and opened his hand to take them.

– You were the one who gave me the note with the list of stamps on, I said angrily. Anyway, why can't I go there? I know the way.

He came up very close to me. His eyes were glaring wildly. He grabbed my cheek and pinched it so hard that it hurt.

– Never, d'you understand? Never on your own.

He walked away. I was amazed he could find the strength to pinch my cheek like that, as he could scarcely stand on his two feet. His long fingers, the same ones that had glided over the keys, were hanging down by his side as if they were lumps of wood. How could someone's fingers be so different from one day to the next?

CHAPTER EIGHT

I heard the school bell ringing and ran so as not to be late, with the pill under my tongue. We had an hour of maths, first lesson.

Mr Benos went straight to the board and began to write with the chalk. His fingers were the same as always, they didn't change from one day to the next: long, stocky fingers, with neatly trimmed short nails.

– Come on Tina, come up and solve this problem for us.

I got up. Or rather, the Other Tina got up, the one who's not bothered about anything. I took the chalk from Mr Benos's hand, though there was a whole pile of chalk next to the board. He looked at me, astonished.

– What are you thinking of, setting us such an easy one, said Cheeky Tina as she wrote out the solution.

– You may have done these exercises before, but there are thirty others in the class who are doing them for the first time, said Mr Benos sternly.

'Am I bothered?' I said to myself, and as soon as the exercise was finished, before Mr Benos could tell me to sit down, I made my way back to my desk.

Vicky looked at me, her eyes wide open.

Mr Benos went back to the board and began to explain the point of today's lesson.

A boy put up his hand. It was Panayotis, bottom of the class.

– Excuse me, Mr Benos, but I can't understand this at all.

– Are you really such a complete twit? said Tina, and the whole class turned and looked, and roared with laughter.

You'd think I just wasn't there for Mr Benos: he ignored me completely, he didn't even look in the direction of my desk. It was as if he was zapping with the remote, and had gone onto another channel. He began to explain from the beginning, talking to Panayoti as if he was the only one in the class. Then he finally asked him:

– So do you understand it now, son?

Panayotis stood up, his cheeks had gone bright red, and he said in a low voice:

– No, I'm sorry, I don't.

– Never mind. It's probably my fault for explaining it in such a confusing way. Now pay attention and I'll make it easy-peasy this time, said Mr Benos.

He began once again to speak in that deep, beautiful voice of his, very slowly, as if he wanted what he was saying to go straight into Panayoti's thick head.

I raised my hand:

– Can I go outside for a moment? I don't feel well.

– Yes, said Mr Benos curtly, with his eyes still focused on Panayoti.

I hurried out of the class, discreetly whisking my bag away with me, and ran straight into the playground. It was empty, the big gate locked. It was only opened at the end of the day. But I simply had to get out of there. We had another hour with Mr Benos after the break, and I didn't want to see him again. No, I wasn't afraid of him. Today I wasn't afraid of anyone. I was absolutely going to get out whatever happened. I'd just had an idea, and I had to tell Wick about it straight away. I couldn't wait till we'd finished school. If I could get out now, I'd run into him somewhere because, of course, he hadn't come to school. I expect he'd got Vinegar Face to give him a sick note, now he had all the money from the other stamps.

I went up to the section of the railings where there was a row of trees on the other side. I threw my bag up so high that it caught in one of the trees. Then I began to clamber over the railings.

Herr Gunther, our gym teacher in Aachen, used to say: 'Even if Tina is last in all the other exercises, she's always first when it comes to climbing up the pole.' And that Tina, the one from Aachen, with the mum and dad and the feather duvet, she was shinning and shinning up the railing like a little monkey, to the amazement of all.

Before I'd realised, I was at the top of the railings and I was almost over the other side. Except that my belt had got caught on one of the spikes.

That was where I was hanging when they found me: Mr Benos, and the headmistress, and the whole school, because at that moment the bell had rung and they'd all come out for break. Shouts, laughter. 'Everyone be quiet!' 'Someone bring a ladder.'

I was watching them from high up and I had the urge to laugh, because I realised how funny I must look. I wasn't scared. As I said, the Other Tina isn't afraid of anything.

My whole class had gathered near the railings, and right at the front was Vicky, shouting up at me anxiously:

– Hold on tight, they're bringing a ladder.

Look at all the kids in my class! Thirty-one if you count me as well, and I haven't made friends with any of them except Vicky, who's mad about this pop singer Kouvas or Rouvas or whatever his name is, and who tells me the storylines of all the Mexican soaps she watches on TV. I guess the reason we get on is because she doesn't ask me about myself, or my parents, or Germany. The other kids who tried to talk to me when I first arrived, they wanted to know everything about me, while Vicky just wanted to tell me about her own stuff.

Funny all that passing through my mind, while I'm hanging from the railings! Perhaps because from up here I'm looking at the kids down there shouting:

– Tina, hold on . . . Mr Benos is coming with the ladder.

Were they really so worried I was going to fall? And Ms Greek Geek, what had got into her? Eyes wide open, utterly terrified. Even little Tamara, the girl from Russia, was covering her mouth with her hands.

It was just that, without my wanting it to, my heart started to pound like mad when I saw the ladder being leant against the railings, saw Mr Benos climbing it, getting up to where I was, taking me in one arm, and with his other hand unhooking my belt, then taking me down the ladder holding me round the waist. He was gripping me tightly, his face had turned grey, the kids down below were applauding and shouting 'Bravo'. The headmistress was calling out: 'Be quiet, get back to your classes', the bell was ringing, then suddenly the playground was empty, apart from the headmistress, Mr Benos, me, and the ladder.

Even then I wasn't afraid of them, even when they took me to the headmistress's study and grilled me: 'Do you realise what you've done?' I'm not saying anything until tomorrow. What am I supposed to say? That I knew very well what I was doing?

– Konstantina, why were you trying to climb over the railings?

– Tell us – you always tell the truth, said Mr Benos, who was trying to sound calm.

– Because the gate was locked, replied the Other Tina, as if she was telling them off for locking it.

The headmistress, who kept taking out her hair slides and putting them back in, the ones with the fake diamonds, froze with her hand in the air.

– This is beyond the limit. I'm going to have to contact her home . . .

– No, don't, said Mr Benos. I'll do that myself. Otherwise her grandmother will have a shock. Let her stay here in your office, and when I've finished the lesson, I'll take her home.

He went out without turning round or looking at me. I remained there with the headmistress. She didn't tell me to sit down.

– I've thrown my bag outside, into the trees.

– I suppose you want me to go and fetch it? Are these the manners they taught you in West Germany?

– It's all 'Germany' now, I corrected her .

– She looked at me as if I'd said a really bad word. Her eyes hardened.

– I'm not going to cane you. We don't hit children here. We're not like the Germans.

– They don't beat anyone, ever, at school in Germany, I said indignantly.

– We'll be excluding you for three days, that's a very short time, considering.

Then she pressed a button on her desk, and after a few minutes Alexandra the canteen lady came in.

– Alexandra, would you please fetch a bag that's stuck in the trees outside the railings, she said, giving her the key to the padlocked front gate.

She spoke to her in a familiar, rather patronising way, as if Alexandra was a child she was talking down to. Wonderful example you're giving us, Ms Boss,

I wanted to say, but didn't dare.

The time seemed to go by incredibly slowly.

Alexandra brought my bag.

– It's lucky it got caught in the tree so nobody took it, said Alexandra, who was standing holding my bag, not knowing what to do with it.

– Leave it on the floor thanks, Alexandra.

Well, at least she said thanks.

– Thank you ever so much, Alexandra, that was very, very kind of you, I said, and I don't know why, but the headmistress gave me a really angry look.

So there we were, the headmistress, me, and my bag. I don't think the time passed quickly for any of us. She was rummaging among some papers she had on her desk, and I shifted my position every now and then while looking at the hands of the large clock on the wall; it was as if they weren't moving at all. My bag sat there patiently, waiting on the floor.

Finally the school bell went. What's all this, Tina? Are you suddenly afraid because Mr Benos is going to take you home? But you're not afraid of anything, I reminded the Other Tina, who grabbed her bag and stood waiting as if nothing at all had happened.

Mr Benos came into the office.

– Let's go, he said, without looking at me.

– Three days exclusion, said the headmistress. I won't give you an official note to take with you, Mr Benos, since you're taking it upon yourself . . .

We went out onto the street. I kicked at a cigarette packet that someone had thrown away. Mr Benos stood still, and so did I.

– Are you feeling OK? I heard his voice saying to me, but it sounded strange, like someone else's voice.

– I'm absolutely fine, I replied, giving the packet a final kick and sending it flying.

– I can see how absolutely fine you are, he said, lifting my chin, so I couldn't avoid looking him straight in the eyes.

That made me snap out of it. I couldn't face Mr Benos's piercing blue eyes without being sorry for what I'd done.

– I . . . don't . . .

That was all I managed to get out.

– Did you ask your grandmother about going to the theatre with the class on Saturday?

– I'm going to the Athens Concert Hall to hear Mozart's Piano Concerto No. 22, said the Other Tina, not looking him in the eyes and screwing up her courage again.

– Are you going with your grandmother?

– Yes, and with her friends, replied Tina the Liar without blushing at all.

– That's a pity, he said, sounding disappointed – we could have had a talk during the interval of the play.

Just before we reached my house, he said again, with a voice that didn't seem at all like him:

– But we will have a talk soon, Tina. You wouldn't climb over those railings if there wasn't something seriously bothering you. And one way or another,

I'm going to find out what it is.

Then once again his voice became the deep, warm voice of the Mr Benos I was used to.

– I've got to find out what's going on inside that shaved head of yours.

We were just outside gran's house.

– Do you want me to come in, or will you tell your grandmother by yourself?

– I'll tell her myself, said the Other Tina, already planning inside that shaved head of hers the lies she was going to tell Farmor.

– I have every confidence that you'll tell her everything. The headmistress didn't give me an official note about the exclusion because I said I'd speak with your gran myself. And by the way, I'm going to ask the head to reduce your exclusion to two days. So you'll be coming back to school on Thursday.

He made as if to go, but then hesitated.

– At the long break on Thursday, wait in class – I'll come along and find you.

– We're not allowed to stay inside.

– I'll get permission from the headmistress. Now go on home.

– Bye, Mr Benos, and thank you, and don't worry . . .

– I am worried, quite a lot actually. Till Thursday.

I waited until he'd walked away, then I rang the bell. Farmor opened the door.

– How come you're back so early?

– I started to cough and cough, and they told me to go home.

– Not more bronchitis! sais Farmor, in despair. And you've spilt all the cough syrup. Lucky there's one left.

– Dad said he's going to send some more.

– I don't see what good that German stuff has done you, she complained and went to get me another bottle.

I went to my room, sat on the bed, and thought it over: if I was kept indoors for two days, I wouldn't be able to meet Wick. I'd have to pretend my cough was gone, and the whole of Wednesday I'd roam the streets until I found him. No use delaying, I had to tell him straight away what was on my mind. As for my German class, Vinegar Face could give me a sick note too. Perhaps Wick would be on good form again, maybe he'd have washed his hair and we'd go back to Navarinou Street so he could play the piano. We'd have the whole of Wednesday to ourselves. He just had to be on good form, that was all . . .

I heard Farmor coming, so I started to cough. I was doing it really well. She brought me the cough mixture.

– Leave it with me, I said, so I don't have to go into the bathroom every hour.

She put her hand on my forehead.

– Hm! You don't have any fever. Lie down though, and I'll bring you something to eat in bed. Some hot vegetable soup and a piece of spinach pie.

I got undressed, put on my pyjamas, snuggled down under the grey blanket, but then I suddenly began to shiver and feel afraid. How on earth did I manage to clamber over the railings? What was I going to say to Mr Benos on Thursday? How was I going to cope until Wednesday, when I was going to get Wick to slip me another pill to give me confidence? Why didn't he give me a whole load so I could keep some in reserve? How was I going to go back to class – how can I face them all? Without a pill I'm just a cowardly little girl with no hair. 'When you don't have anything else, drink the cough syrup and that'll calm you down.' He knows everything, does Mr Wick. But I don't want to calm down. I just want to think about absolutely nothing, nothing at all. 'I'm sorry, Farmor, I've spilt it again.' 'Whatever you say, Ismeni, I'm convinced something's wrong with that child.' Little Demi was getting a bee in her bonnet.

– Why have you covered yourself up like that? Sit up and eat your soup!

I sat up in bed. Farmor rested the tray on my knees, and gave me a spoonful of syrup. A single spoonful! As soon as she'd turned her back, I drank down half the bottle. I just wanted to drift into nothingness, not to think about this coming Thursday, and Mr Benos . . . and Aachen.

I finished the soup and put the tray on the floor. Of course I couldn't eat the spinach pie. I huddled down under the grey blanket again and felt a gentle drowsiness, but without wanting to go to sleep. I could hear some water flowing somewhere. That'd be dad shaving, and he's left the bathroom door open . . .

I pulled back the blanket a bit, to uncover my face. What had got into Herr Heiner, for him to come out in the afternoon, to walk on his little treadmill? Krrrr, krrrr. If only you could have seen me today, Herr Heiner, high up there on the railings. And you, the real Herr Heiner, if only you could have seen Tina with her stong-willed, determined look.

– Aren't you going to eat the spinach pie?

I opened my eyes and saw Farmor pick up the tray from the floor. She turned round to leave.

– Please shut the door.

– I'm going to leave it open, in case you need anything.

– I don't need anything.

– You don't know that . . .

The door wide open. Krrrr, krrrr, water tap in the bathroom. No, no one in the bathroom, and it's not my dad shaving, it's Herr Heiner spinning his wheel.

– How are you?

– How are you?

– How are you?

One by one the Demetrias put their heads round the door. I must have fallen asleep, and didn't hear them arrive.

– I'm fine, I say and remember to cough.

– Just get better, and on Sunday, if it's sunny like today, we'll go for a drive, says Smart Demi.

– Coffee's ready, calls Farmor from the kitchen, and the three heads disappear again.

Oh, those outings with Farmor and the Demis! I used to wish it would rain on Sundays, but as if it was doing it on purpose, the sun would always be shining brightly. 'The newspaper says sunshine in Athens', mum would say sadly as she looked through the window at the densely falling snow in Aachen. But dad and I liked to have walks in the snow.

And now, excursions in the sunshine . . . Smart Demi in charge:

– Let's go to Kaisariani.

Little Demi at the steering wheel. Arriving, piling out of the car.

And now Tina, who knows nothing about anything, has to learn everything.

– These were the execution grounds.

– In the Occupation, the Germans used to shoot Greek patriots here, sometimes 200 on a single day.

– Stop kicking stones around and pay attention to what we're telling you.

Farmor, plucking at my sleeve.

Another Sunday, somewhere else.

– You see those marks on the walls?

– That's from the mortars the British aimed at us in December '44, when we had the uprising.

Yet another Sunday.

– Here where the Supreme Court is, this is where the old Averof Prison used to be.

– We all passed through here.

– There was a little courtyard with a single tree in the middle. A palm-tree.

And still another Sunday.

– This is Bouboulina Street. Right here was the building where they used to torture people during the military dictatorship, in the late 1960s and early 1970s. But they've pulled that down now as well.

Searching for my headphones, so I can listen to Silver Moon. Trying to get them out of the little rucksack I take along to use as a handbag. A hand stopping me. Farmor's hand.

Even now her hand is as beautiful as it was back then in the photograph, holding the rifle.

Once more I'm tangled up in the spiders' webs. Struggling to get free. Just a few more Sundays . . . let it rain just once . . . And then put my plan into action . . . to find Wick as quickly as possible, and to write to Sigrid.

Dear Tinopoula,

Why don't you want a mobile phone? Your dad can send you one and he says he'll pay the phone bills. How pig-headed you've become . . .

You've no idea, Sigrid. Why should I get a mobile? So Farmor can get hold of me? On the other hand, I could use it to track down Wick. But he doesn't have a mobile. He had one when he came here from Cologne, but his mum took it away because she said he was running up bills.

The Demis are chattering away with gran at the other end of the house. They're talking about Sunday. Making plans for me. And me, I'm making plans for myself and Wick . . .

CHAPTER NINE

Next morning, I leapt out of bed and ran into the kitchen, where Farmor was sitting.

– How are you, then? Do you want your milk?

– I'm fine, I think I'll go to school.

Wait until the second lesson, at least. Let the day get a bit warmer before you set off. I'll write you a note.

Good idea, because I certainly wouldn't find Wick on the streets this early in the morning. Shouldn't think he's suddenly decided to go to school today!

Ten o'clock . . . No kid with a school bag can be seen wandering through the streets at this time of day, other than the little kids from the nursery school, that is. And Tina.

Not little Tina from Aachen, the one with the mum, the dad, the feather duvet, the wolf without a soul, the four horses at the railway station and all the other stuff.

And not that Tina who dreamed of becoming a horsewoman, an ice dancer, the one who strolled in the Annastrasse with her dad, before everything turned upside down, nor the pupil with the 'determined look' at Herr Heiner's school, who sat next to him at the *Café Roncalli* and ate apple strudel and made him promises.

This Tina, hanging around Kypseli looking for Wick, is the same one who shinned up the school railings and lied through her teeth, even to Mr Benos, who had only ever been nice to her.

Wick had vanished into thin air. I went and stood outside the door of the block of flats where Lady Di was living.

Wick appeared at a quarter to eleven on the dot. Not from the street. He came out of the building. He didn't see me straight away. His hair was dirty and matted. He was holding in his hands what looked like a shoebox.

– Hi, I said.

He turned and saw me.

What are you doing here?

– I was looking for you. Don't worry, I'm not going up there. I was waiting in case you turned up.

– You didn't go to school today? I heard all about your doings yesterday. Alexandra told me; she's a neighbour of ours, she was at my mother's. A shame I wasn't there, to see you hanging from the railings. What were you doing up there?

– I had to get out to try and find you, and they'd padlocked the gate.

– But didn't I gave you a pill before lessons?

– Yup, you did.

– Look, don't overdo it, because . . . you know what happens afterwards.

I interrupted, telling him that I'd wanted to see him because I had a big plan, that we could only put into practice if we worked together.

Something started to scrabble around inside the box he was holding.

– What have you got in there?

– A little owl. It fell onto Lady Di's veranda. I'm going to take it to Aegina.

– The island of Aegina? What are you going to do with it there?

I was amazed, but also worried he'd leave before I could tell him my plan.

– The owl has a broken wing – they'll be able to treat it there, at the wildlife hospital.

I'd come up with an entire plan, and he was talking about owls! I held him back forcibly by the sleeve.

– Please, you have to listen to me, I said, and only just stopped myself bursting into tears.

– But it'll die, I have to take it there quickly. Right now I can . . . I don't know about later on.

– What don't you know? I asked fearfully.

He looked at me and his eyes changed – like when he was playing the piano. He began to speak to me in German, as if there was someone nearby who wasn't to hear what it was we were discussing. His voice didn't break like it did when he spoke Greek, and he spoke continuously, not just in a few broken phrases.

He said he owed it to the little owl to save its life, because it had saved him, for today at least. He was just about to find a vein – and I shouldn't pretend not to understand, he was sure I knew very well what he was intending to do. Even when he was a little boy, the doctor used to have trouble because his veins were so deep down under the skin. He hadn't been able to locate one. Lady Di tried, too. Finally, he decided to look for one in his leg. Losing patience, he'd gone out onto the veranda and sat on the ground, so he was hidden from the houses opposite by the pots with their large plants. He'd taken off his socks, and just as was stretching out his bare leg, something fell on top of him. It was the little owl. He dropped the rubber strap and took the bird in his hands. Its wing was broken. He'd read in a magazine somewhere that they give medical treatment to injured birds on Aegina. He really loved birds . . . and particularly owls. Back in Cologne, he had a whole pile of books on birds and knew all the different kinds. He'd even kept an owl of his own at home, called Electra. He'd found it when he was with his father in a forest where they'd gone for a bike ride. One of its wings was broken, and although they'd taken it to an owl doctor, he couldn't heal it. They took it home. It could scarcely manage to fly from the lowest shelf of the bookcase. If they'd left it in the forest, it would have died. So they kept it. His father called it Electra, because it used to let out cries like an actress he'd seen in the ancient Greek theatre at Epidauros, where they were putting on the tragedy *Electra*. At that time he'd been seeing a lot of his father.

Meanwhile Lady Di had got really stressed out.

– I hope you don't think I'm going to wait all day.

She grabbed hold of the rubber strap and in an instant she'd injected herself in the arm. She's got incredible veins, apparently.

– Nobody could have stopped me once I had the rubber strap on. Only the owl, which reminded me straight away of Electra. My father told me when we were leaving that he'd look after it. But I don't believe anything he says any more.

He stopped and bent over the box to listen to the bird moving around.

It really cheered me up that he was telling me about himself, about his life. It meant I'd be able to tell him my plan. In German. Since that's our language. We'd spoken it all day at school. All our games we'd played in German. And the songs, and our books outside school, the ones with stories and fairy tales, they'd all been in German.

– Come to Aegina with me and we can talk on the boat, he said.

I'd never been to Aegina before. I know it's not far from Athens. But Farmor and her friends had never taken me there on an outing to show me the prisons. I expect they're keeping it for the summer. I'm sure they don't know the island has a sanctuary that treats sick owls.

I decided to go with him . . .

– I'll phone my gran and tell her . . . that Greek Geek has kept us in for rehearsals for the play she wants us to put on at the end of the year. That I didn't know because I was away yesterday . . . and that I'll be going straight on to my German class. I hope Vinegar Face can give me a note to cover my absences.

Wick gave me a phone card.

– Won't you get worn out? asked Farmor.

– No, I'm feeling OK.

– Are you coming by to collect your books for German?

– Won't be able to manage it in the time. Bye.

I put down the phone before she got anything else in.

Until six o'clock, with Wick and the owl on Aegina, I'd have time to tell him everything.

We took the old metro to Piraeus. I hated it. Such a crush of people. We had to stand up. Wick was worrying the whole time that the owl might start scratching around in its box. The lid was full of holes, but every so often he opened it a fraction and looked inside. I decided I'd talk to him on the ship, as all he was concerned with was the owl. He paid for the tickets. He said he had some money left over from the stamps. That was lucky, because I only had enough money with me for a cheese pasty.

On the boat, Wick didn't want us to go down into the saloon. We stayed on the deck, under cover.

– Aren't we going to get very cold when it gets going? I was a bit anxious, although the sun was shining and there was very little wind.

– We'll pull up our hoods. I can't stand the saloons

they have on these boats. Makes me feel suffocated, said Wick, and drawing up two white plastic chairs, he put them very close to the ship's railing. If it got windy, we'd sit down on the deck.

I didn't say a word, just sat down next to him. The ship moved off. The noise from the engine was quite loud. In order to make myself heard, I had to shout. Why didn't he want us to go down to the saloon? How could I find the nerve to tell him what I wanted to if I had to yell? I waited for him to stop fussing over the owl, to take some notice of me, but he carried on fiddling with the lid of the box, opening it and then half-shutting it over and over again. I couldn't stand waiting any longer, but as soon as I began to speak in German, I realised I wouldn't need any pills.

My tongue ran away with me, and I told him everything in one go, as loudly as I could, almost right into his ear, so he wouldn't miss a word amidst the din of the ship's engine.

– You know . . . I was thinking we could leave. Go back to Germany. You to Cologne, me to Aachen. I'll find the best stamps to pay for our airfares.

Hadn't his Headteacher written to offer to take him in? He should reply immediately, and I'd write to Sigrid. She has a second bed in her room. I wouldn't go and live with mum or with dad. I'd wait for mum to give birth to Mr Michalis's baby – OK then, my little half-brother. And for both my parents to find larger homes, and once they'd managed to 'work out their problems more calmly' as Herr Heiner said, then they could decide what they'd do with me. Here in Athens, we're both going round the bend. Lying, playing truant, popping pills, rubber straps, veins . . .

I stopped and waited to see what effect I'd had on him. I stared straight ahead at the sea. I didn't turn round to look at him: all I knew was that he wasn't saying anything, just fumbling with the box.

Silence. Just the drone of the ship's engine. Oh, please let him speak. Say something. Anything.

– We'd have to do it straight away, he said suddenly, just when I'd given up on him replying at all.

I hung on his every word.

– I can't expect some owl or other to come along every day and stop me . . . soon nothing will be able to stop me.

– We'll write the letters tomorrow, no later. No, wait, we'll do it this evening, and send them express, and I'll find a way to creep into Farmor's room and pick out the best stamps.

He agreed! I hadn't expected it to be so easy. I wanted to get up and dance out of sheer joy. But his face was dark and gloomy.

– You think we can manage it?

– Of course we can. I mean, how long can it take for the letters to get there and come back?

– I meant the owl, can we manage it so it doesn't croak?

We got off the ferry and Wick said we should take a taxi. Pity – I wanted to have a walk along the marina, past the yachts and little dinghies, so we could talk about our plans.

There were lots of taxis, and one stopped right in front of us. Wick sat next to the driver. I didn't think it was very polite of him, leaving me to sit in the back on my own.

– To the prison, I heard him say, and it made me jump.

– What did you say? I almost yelled at him, grabbing his shoulder.

– Don't shriek like that, he said without turning his head. That's where they look after the birds.

Then he started a conversation with the driver. You'd think there was nobody at all sitting in the back. He told him about the little owl, as if the taxi driver was his best mate.

– You've got here just in time, said the driver. They've just allocated them a place up on the mountain and most of the animals have already been transferred there.

From behind I could study Wick's head and his dirty hair – this time he'd tied it up with a shoelace. I didn't want to travel around with him like that. He ought to wash his hair, he ought to talk to me.

– Here we are, said the taxi driver. I'll set you down here – the road is in a terrible state from here on.

We got out. The taxi drove off. We walked on for a bit – not talking, of course. Next to the sea, there was a building made out of blocks of stone. It was long and narrow, with small windows in a row, all of them covered with iron bars and with wire-mesh on the inside.

– Why did they put the birds in a prison? I ventured to ask, but got no reply.

We looked for the entrance to the building and found the courtyard. It wasn't very big; it was paved, with high walls around it. There were storks strolling up and down it, but they weren't at all disturbed that we'd suddenly appeared before them. There were some with moulting feathers, and some with bandaged feet.

Wick found the entrance and I followed him in, then down a long passageway. At the bottom there was a little door – locked. He knocked, and a girl opened it.

– Come in, I see you've brought a new patient! she said.

She took the shoebox out of Wick's hands and put it on a table.

We were in a small room full of large cardboard boxes, and from inside them came the sound of high-pitched little voices. On the table were little medicine bottles, scissors, and little bowls with a reddish liquid in which various implements were soaking, just like at the dentist's.

The girl opened the box and took the owl in her hands. I saw it for the first time. How beautiful it was! It had a little grey head, with tiny wings in the shape of a hood, and white feathers like a ribbon beneath its chin. The girl caught hold of its broken wing, and it gave out a faint cry like a baby.

– Oh you poor little thing, what did they do to you?

Wick told the girl what happened – not the whole story, obviously – and the girl looked again very carefully at the wing that was hanging down.

– We'll do what we can. I'm just afraid that it won't ever fly properly again. What a pity, it's such a beautiful little bird!

Then she put the owl against her cheek.

– What's your name, my sweet?

– Tina. It was Wick who'd said it. My heart began to pound as if it would never stop.

The girl kissed its head.

– Well, my name is Katerina. In a short while Elsa will be here. She's our doctor and she'll take care of you.

– What will happen to it? asked Wick.

– If it does finally recover, we'll send it back into the forest. If not, we'll keep it here with its cousins.

– In prison? I asked anxiously.

Katerina repeated what the taxi driver had already told us: they'd been granted a large area on the mountain and they'd already started to take a lot of the animals there. They just kept the birds here, and soon they'd be going too.

– But why did you put them in a prison? I dared to ask again.

Katerina isn't like Wick: she gave me a straight answer when I asked her a question. She said that when the prison had been closed, the buildings stayed empty for a long time. Finally, they allowed them to shelter the injured animals and birds there; until then they'd been kept in various places, even in the carers' houses. At first there weren't that many, but when people found out about it, birds began to arrive unexpectedly from all over the place. Mainly injured and sick birds that no one else would take in.

– Here's Elsa now . . .

In the doorway stood a very slim girl with short, flaming-red hair. Katerina put the owl into her hands.

– Look, these guys have brought it from Athens, it was injured when they found it. It's called Tina.

Elsa said she'd do what she could, and Katerina took us to see where the birds lived.

If only Farmor and the Demetrias could have seen me roaming about the place where the prisoners used to be all crammed together, as Katerina told us.

Through the tiny windows came only a single ray of light. For human beings, it must have been awful to live in the semi-darkness, but the owls, perched on the logs of trees in the middle of a gigantic wire cage, imagined it was night-time, so they had their eyes wide open. There were small owls just like the one we'd brought along, with their little hoods fringed by a white ribbon at the chin.

Next to them, separated by wire, were gigantic great owls. On their heads were thick, bushy wings, lying there like withered leaves.

Further on, in another cage, sitting on imitation rocks, were eagles with half-closed eyes, letting out a cry every so often.

Wick's attention had been caught by another cage in the corner of the building, where huge vultures were sitting, pinned down with chains, not moving at all, as if they'd been enchanted by an evil witch who had put them to sleep for a hundred years, just like in the fairy story.

– So this is where our owl – I didn't dare say the name 'Tina' – will be kept, if it can't learn to fly again?

– As I said, we're transferring them to the mountain, replied Katerina. Soon a lorry-load will be leaving for there. We're transferring some of the babies that have fallen out of their nests. Come with me and see where your Tina will be living.

When we got outside and I had to face the heat and the sun, I felt as if I'd been nursing my own wings, and now I was able to fly. Did Farmor and the three Demetrias really spend years and years of their lives in prisons like this one? Without ever seeing the light of day, like birds with broken wings, unable to fly free out into the air, to the outside world? I glanced at Wick out of the corner of my eye. He was squinting, as if he'd spent years inside this prison as well.

Outside on the road we saw a small lorry. Katerina told us to get in and wait for her. When she came back, she was carrying a large cardboard box.

Wick got down, took it from her, and put it next to me in the bed of the lorry. Inside it were little grey birds, lying higgledy-piggledy on top of one another.

– These are my babies, said Katerina. Little owls who've fallen out of the nest.

She climbed into the lorry with Wick.

– Oh, if only I had an assistant, I wish I wish, we need more help. What do you say, would you like to come in the summer to work as volunteers?

– We're not going to be . . . I began to say, but Wick nudged me in the ribs with his elbow, and I shut up.

From the road, someone was approaching on a bicycle. He had long untidy hair, and on his shoulder sat a large parrot with moulting feathers.

– Hey, Argyris, Katerina called to him. You'll have to take us up to the mountain. I've got some visitors as well.

– Volunteers, volunteers, we need more help, said the parrot, and we all began to laugh.

– Shut up, Captain, said Katerina. I see you're still taking down everything I say.

Argyris got down off the bicycle, and with the parrot still on his shoulder, climbed into the cab and started up the motor.

We set off. We left the sea behind us, going more and more uphill all the time. We passed fields with pistachio trees, then bare hillocks, until the lorry stopped in front of a fence. Argyris got down and dragged open a large iron gate.

We got down too. Wick picked up the box of fledglings and we followed Katerina into a little house with a tiled roof. In front of it there was a small veranda covered with straw matting. Katerina told Wick where to put the box, and we noticed that the cottage was the only one that had been finished. All around us were half-completed buildings, in a large area strewn with rocks. Here and there a shrub broke through. Not a single tree anywhere to be seen. Far below, the sea stretched away, a deep deep blue.

We sat on the parapet wall of the courtyard, and Katerina described the trees and flowers they were going to plant. Then she excused herself, explaining she was going to have to take care of her 'babies', and Argyris carried the box into the house.

– I shan't be long, she called, as she went into the house. Meanwhile you can take a walk round our little kingdom.

I stayed alone with Wick, and we went to take a look at the buildings, which didn't yet have any roofs, or doors, or windows.

We went into a big open space, long and narrow, where the whole of one wall had gaping holes through which you could glimpse the sea.

– If they put the birds here, ours won't have a bad time at all, I remarked to Wick, who hadn't said a single word to me since we arrived on Aegina.

Yet he'd called the owl Tina – that was enough.

Suddenly he began to speak:

– I should stay here . . . with the birds, he said in a faraway voice, gazing out to sea.

– But we're leaving for Germany. You promised.

– Fine . . . You just need to get those stamps first, he snapped, and my pulse returned to normal.

As we went back to the cottage, we saw a giant eagle in the back garden. It wasn't moving at all. It must be stuffed, I thought. Further on, hanging onto a chain with its claws, there was an incredibly beautiful black bird, with one wing like a folded-up fan, with a long slender beak curved at the tip . . . It looked as if it was made of marble too.

– It's a cormorant, said Wick, who seemed to know all about birds. But what the hell are they here for? Have those birds been stuffed?

I felt dreadfully sad – I realised that if our little Tina didn't recover, she might end up like that, too. Wick seemed to have the same thought, because when he turned I saw the anger in his eyes. Then I wondered if I was seeing things, because the cormorant's wing began to open slowly, like a giant fan.

I was terrified. I grabbed hold of Wick's arm. His golden eyes were blinking in alarm. At the same moment we saw the 'stuffed' eagle spread out two immense wings that cast a shadow over the scrub and rocks all around, while the eagle remained motionless in its place. We looked at one another in amazement.

Katerina came out of the door and saw us.

– Poor things, she said. They're blind, someone shot them in the eyes. That's why they can't fly.

– Blind people can walk around if someone takes their hand, or with a stick, or with a dog to guide them, said Wick, his voice wavering.

– People, yes, but not birds. Doesn't matter how strong their wings are, without their eyes they're rooted to the ground, said Katerina sadly.

Then she explained how the cormorant normally dives into the water to fish for its food. Now they bring the fish to it in a basin of water, but even then they have to feed the fish into its mouth by hand. And the eagle stays still on its rock, and we have to catch it by its wing so it can take a couple of steps.

The cormorant opened and closed its useless wings. Wick went up to it and stroked its jet-black feathers.

We got ready to leave. Katerina had to stay and look after her chicks. Argyris would take us to the harbour. We got up into the lorry. He was already at the wheel, with the parrot on his shoulder. Katerina came to say goodbye.

– Volunteers, volunteers, we need more help, cried the parrot.

– He's right, we'll be expecting you back here some day, said Katerina, dragging open the heavy iron gates.

Luckily, we took the hovercraft for the return journey, so as not to be late. While we were waiting for it, Wick gave me a pill. I swallowed it straight away. He reckoned I'd need it to get through my ordeal with Farmor. It was nice that he was thinking of me. But once we sat down in our seats, he didn't say a word until we arrived. And I wanted so much to talk about the blind cormorant, and the eagle, and our little Tina, who might never fly again. And about our own journey to freedom.

CHAPTER TEN

I got back home on the dot of six. As soon as she opened the door, Farmor asked me if I had a fever.

– Your cheeks are bright red.

– I was running just now on the street, I said, slipping straight back into lying. I hadn't realised that my cheeks had caught the sun and the wind.

– D'you have a big part in the play?

– Which play?

– The one you're rehearsing for.

I didn't reply, and Farmor had to ask me three times.

– Not many lines, I said finally, and went to my room.

As soon as I'd put down my bag, I glanced at Herr Heiner's cage and felt a sudden twinge of remorse. What would happen to him when I left? Farmor definitely wouldn't keep him, and I couldn't see her giving him to the Kurdish refugees. No, she wouldn't even give him to the cat to eat, and the cat wouldn't thank her if she did. What about Little Demi? I'd leave her a letter. I'm sure she'd give him a home . . . as long as our plan to run away succeeded. I'd just have to find a way of being here on my own so I could look for the stamps.

The telephone rang, and I opened the door to listen. It might be dad.

– Yes . . . yes . . . what, such a long time? said Farmor, and at first I couldn't work out who it was on the phone. Yes, Tina's here, you can talk to her, but tell me about it first . . . She was absolutely fine with Tina, and now she has to stay in bed until the last moment . . . What a worry it all is . . .

I threw myself on the phone and snatched it out of gran's hand.

– What's wrong with mum?

– Calm down . . . she just needs to be careful . . . she has to stay in bed until the baby is born . . . Otherwise everything's OK, she's fine. Tell me what you're up to.

– Mum has never had a day's illness in her life, and you always told me that when I was born . . .

– It's all OK . . . OK . . . And my leg is nearly as good as new. Nearly 100 per cent.

– You're always saying 'nearly'.

– Look, Tina love, don't worry . . . everything's going to be absolutely fine . . . Mum's going to call you as well.

Serves me right for not liking Mr Michalis's baby. Now mum is stuck in bed. Mum, who never sits still for an instant. 'You're whirling around like a spinning top!' dad used to tease her. Let me get away from here soon, so I can go and be with her . . .

After we'd eaten, I lay down on my bed, and felt

that tiredness once more. I'm great at the start, once I've swallowed the pill down, I can climb over railings and everything. But as time passes, my legs begin to shake and I lose it completely. What on earth do those pills have in them? First they take me up to the top of the mountain and then I come crashing back down. Just like the mountaineer I saw in a documentary on television. He'd stuck a steel peg into the rock he was climbing up, and he was making fast his rope, and all of a sudden he was down in the ravine at the bottom. I won't take any more pills, I promise, but as soon as I think about what I have to face, I forget all my promises and go looking for Wick.

It's Thursday tomorrow. Back to school. What if he's not waiting around for me at one corner or another to give me a pill?

I'm gripped by fear. How can I face Mr Benos at break, and what will I tell him? I'm afraid . . . about mum . . . about everything. I feel cold, and I cover myself up with the blanket, my head too.

Herr Heiner is turning his wheel, all happy-happy. He doesn't know what's ahead of him.

I can't go to sleep – something's going to happen. I feel as if my head will explode with all these problems. I wrap myself in the bedclothes again. Luckily, there's still the bottle of syrup on the bedside table. There's a bit less than half of it left. I'll drink it all down. 'The bottle fell out of my hands, and it spilt.' 'Always so careless.' OK, Farmor, you'll soon be rid of me. That'll be nice for you . . .

I'm not thinking about anything . . . Gradually I drift off to sleep . . .

Farmor woke me for school.

The first lessons went by with Greek Geek. I wasn't paying any attention, I was half asleep. Twice she came up to me and asked if I was all right.

The bell went. Vicky grabbed my hand to go outside.

– I can't. Mr Benos wants to see me at break.

– What's he want?

– How do I know?

– Get it over with quick, so you can come out. I've got some really exciting news. I went to Rouvas's concert, said Vicky, and she went out of the classroom, all lit up.

I stayed on my own. I'd never noticed before how horrible an empty classroom looks. I heard steps in the corridor. I thought I was going to faint. I'd have looked really pale, if my cheeks weren't still red from yesterday's outing.

– Hi there Tina.

He sat down next to me at the desk, just like a fellow-pupil.

– Did your granny give you a hard time for your exclusion?

– Not too bad, I said, making it up on the spot.

– Good, I'm glad. I've come to find out what's been going on with you recently.

Questions, questions, and more questions – I stayed silent. It's not easy to make up lies for Mr

Benos. Suddenly though, I thought of something true I could tell him.

– My mum isn't well.

– What's wrong with her? he asked, with concern.

– She's expecting a baby, Mr Michalis's baby . . . and she has to stay in bed until it's born, and I'm scared.

He put his hand on my head and tried to console me. He told me that happens to a lot of women. And then, just as I thought I'd got it over with, he looked me straight in the eye and said:

– I don't think that's the only thing that's bothering you, Konstantina. I'm not going to put pressure on you now, because we don't have a lot of time and I can see you're worried about your mum, but we'll find an opportunity so you can tell me all about it, bit by bit, and you'll feel better, you'll see.

– Yes, Mr Benos, I said, relieved.

He left me to go out for break. When I reached the door, he called out to me:

– Promise we'll talk?

I turned my head and looked at him, and I wasn't afraid. Soon I'd be gone for ever. I could make a promise.

– Promise, I said, and left quickly, so he wouldn't see the tears pricking my eyes, because I'd fooled him.

Everything went to plan, even faster than Wick was expecting. I sent my letter to Sigrid and her reply came back straight away:

Dear Tinopoula,

OK, you don't need a mobile, you don't need e-mail, as now we'll be sorting it all out pronto. I'm trying to understand, I'm still trying to get my head round all your crazy plans. You say you want to come to Aachen to stay at my place, you make me swear not to tell anyone, so you can surprise your mum and dad . . . So, do you have a school break, then? It's very cold here, ten below zero. But you say you've recovered from your bronchial problems. How can I really keep a secret from your mum? OK, I won't tell anyone - not even the horses at the station. They'll see you come back, and they'll start to gallop from sheer amazement. It was a bit confusing the way you explained it: you'll be arriving alone, but you'll have a friend with you as far as Cologne. Don't tell me - you've fallen in love, and you're running off with him, and leaving him behind in Cologne, because you don't want to turn up in Aachen with him! So I expect later on you'll want us to go there together to fetch him? But what are we going to do with him? I'm dying of curiosity. How did you get to know him? Maybe on some ocean liner - he saved you from the storm, but unlike our precious Leonardo di Caprio he didn't drown? I can't believe it's just some schoolboy with spots.

I don't know what's happened to all the boys in our class: They've all got acne, apart from Diagora. But maybe he has black pimples and you just can't see them. You say I shouldn't phone you because you can't talk in front of your gran - it makes me laugh that you call her Farmor. But is she really so bad-tempered that you're scared of her?

When you come here, you can meet my sweet little Mormor, who's visiting us and staying for a month or so. Where do you want to sleep? On the top bunk bed or the bottom one? Or maybe we can put the mattresses on the floor - because how can we chat properly if one of us is up on top and the other down below? I'm expecting your final message about how and when you're going to get here, and I can't wait to get to know your boy-friend. But if I don't like him, I'll tell you straight out, just like you told me when I liked the boy in the pizzeria. You say you look like a seal with your hair shaved off. I saw the seal the other day when I went past the zoo. His hair's grown back and right now he looks a sorry sight. I'M WAITING FOR YOU. NO WORD TO ANYONE! The biggest secret of our lives. I LIKE IT . . .

X X X
love Sigrid

Now we're just waiting for the reply from Wick's Headteacher in Cologne. But there's a big problem getting the stamps, because Farmor has caught a bad cold from going to visit her Kurds one day, when it was pouring with rain – honestly, you'd think she'd done it on purpose. Now she can't leave the house. The Demis have come, to keep her company and do her shopping. The other day I heard her say to Smart Demi: ' What's up with Tina? Every hour on the hour she comes and asks me how I am!' 'It's because deep down she loves you,' they told her. 'D'you think so?' replied Farmor, and called me in so we could have tea together, as if she wanted to check it out.

To tell the truth, I was trying to be on my very best behaviour, and one day when all three Demis were gathered together, I even asked them to tell me about the man with the strange name that the military had killed, way back during the dictatorship in the late 1960s. They were pleased that I wanted to know.

– It was Elis Panayotis, they said.

They started to tell me all about him, but I was dreaming about the route we'd planned to take, Wick had described it to me in detail. He'd got some information from a travel agency. We'd get the plane to Frankfurt, then get the train. He'd get off at Cologne, and about an hour later I'd reach Aachen.

I'd get out of the train and the four horses would be waiting for me. I'd take the bus and get off close to Sigrid's house . . .

– He was the military junta's first victim.

– Who? I asked in surprise.

– Elis, of course – they killed him at the Racecourse Stadium. The Colonels rounded up a load of people just after they seized power, said Little Demi.

At last! Farmor's cold was better and once again she left Big Demi to do the cooking, because she was going with the others to take Little Demi's nephew, who's a doctor, to treat the Kurds.

I knew Big Demi wouldn't budge from the kitchen until she'd rolled out the sheets of filo pastry for the chicken pies. So I had some time until she put them in the oven.

I sneaked into Farmor's room, having turned the music up loud in my own room, so Big Demi would think I was there. I couldn't look for the stamps one by one. I opened the album and took out whole sheets with the ones that I thought looked the most unusual. But would they be enough?

Next day, Wick was nowhere to be seen, and there I was running round with the stamps in my school bag. I skived off my German class, of course. I looked for him everywhere. If he puts a rubber strap round his leg today, where will he find an owl to save him? He'd promised me that until we left he wouldn't do anything. And besides, he had no money, just a pill to keep him going – that's what he said. I wouldn't need a pill or anything else. I was just anxious that nothing should happen to ruin our plan.

Again, the following day, no sign of him.

Finally, on the third day, just as I was coming home from school, I found him waiting for me at the corner of the street.

– Where have you been? I complained.

– Have you brought the stamps?

He didn't speak to me in German. I could only get a few words out of him. I handed him the stamps. He took them and made as if to go.

– Don't disappear on me again.

– Day after tomorrow, same time, here.

– Do you think the money will be enough? I asked, uncertainly.

– How should I know? he replied, sounding completely stressed out, and he practically ran off.

I wanted to call out to him to stop, so we could talk about our journey. But I realised that Wick couldn't handle any discussions. I was afraid he'd put the rubber strap round his leg again. Even though he'd promised me he wouldn't.

As soon as he'd gone, I wanted to forget about that Wick and just remember the other one, the one with the washed, wavy hair, the colour of honey. How would I get through one more day? How long would it be until that 'day after tomorrow' when I'd find out more?

Wick hadn't told me if he'd heard back from his Headteacher. Perhaps he had. But when he's not on good form, he can scarcely say more than a word or two. He'd better be on good form soon, otherwise . . .

On the street near home, I met Mr Benos. He was with a girl. Tall, pretty, with long chestnut-blonde hair reaching down to her waist. They were holding hands. I tried to pretend not to see them.

– Tina.

Mr Benos's deep voice made my head spin.

Come and meet Marina . . . my girlfriend.

The girl gave me a hug.

– Vasilis has told me so much about you.

So Mr Benos was called Vasilis, and had a girlfriend he'd talked to about me. I was lost for words.

– Tina, my dear, I can see Marina likes you as much as I do. Come to our house on Sunday, and you can see some of her work – she paints wonderful pictures. I'll come and collect you. Tell your grandmother.

Come on, Tina, say something, I urged myself. I was trying hard to think of something, but I couldn't. By Sunday I might not be here.

And I really did want to go to their house. Vasilis and Marina. I'd remember them when I got to Aachen. The only ones I would remember. Perhaps Greek Geek just a bit, too.

– OK, I'll tell my grandmother . . .

– Don't be put off, she's not always this shy. She has a really sharp brain, said Mr Benos – Vasilis, that is – to Marina.

– It's because she's just met me for the first time. We'll get to know each other, and I'm sure we'll become friends. If you'd like to, Tina?

– Yes, I'd like that, I responded, and it was the first time I felt sad about leaving.

The 'day after tomorrow' took ages to arrive. I didn't have any more syrup to help me block it all out. I went to find Wick. Strange, he was actually there where he'd said he'd be, waiting for me. Was that good or bad?

– We've got enough money, he said, without

emotion.

I wanted to throw my arms round his neck and kiss him, but I held myself back.

– Did you hear back from your Headteacher? I asked, nervously.

– Yes, I did. We're leaving the day after tomorrow.

It was as if he'd got stuck on 'the day after tomorrow'. He couldn't have said it more curtly, either. It was as if he didn't care.

– The day after tomorrow! – I was so thrilled.

– Don't shout, he growled at me.

Oh, Wick, I just hope you wash your hair before we leave . . . and speak German to me . . .

– Now listen to what I'm telling you. I'll wait for you in the morning, when you go to school, down in St George's Square. It's far enough away from your home, and from the school. The plane leaves at ten to twelve. We'll get a taxi.

– Have we got enough money for a taxi to the airport?

– Now you're just asking stupid questions, he said, and turned his back on me.

And then he left. And I wanted so much to go to *The Atrium* with him, to drink a hot chocolate and talk as we had done on the boat. I couldn't stand him being so rude to me, having a go at me like that – but then he'd named his owl 'Tina' after me, hadn't he? I wondered if he'd phoned to ask for news of it? But I didn't dare ask him.

The day after tomorrow! Two days from now, I'd

be sleeping next to Sigrid.

The day after tomorrow! It'll be enough if Wick just washes his hair.

CHAPTER ELEVEN

The 'day after tomorrow' – that's today.

I sat up in bed and looked around my room, my cage, for the last time. Herr Heiner was sleeping the sleep of the just. It was lucky he didn't come out of his little hutch to say goodbye, because I'd have burst into tears. I'd written my letter to Little Demi. I'd written one to Farmor as well. Before I leave, I'll find an opportunity to go to the kitchen. Farmor drinks her coffee before I get up, and then doesn't drink any more until four in the afternoon, sometimes even later, when the three Demetrias come round and they all drink coffee together. She keeps it in a brass container with a picture of the Kremlin painted on the outside, and a red star on the lid. I'll pop my letter inside, and by the time she finds it, I'll be gone.

For lunchtime, when she was expecting me home, I'd concocted another lie – I hoped it was the last I was going to tell in my whole life – that I'd be staying at school to do rehearsals with Greek Geek. 'Don't get rubbish from the canteen again, I'll make you a sandwich,' Farmor told me last night, as soon as she heard I wasn't coming home at midday.

From Aachen I'd write a long letter to Mr Benos explaining everything. I'd send greetings to Marina and ask her to phone Aegina to ask about an owl called Tina.

I got up and dressed quickly. I put several books in my bag with my passport, my maths exercise book and Sigrid's letters. The cereals and milk were waiting for me on the breakfast table. The last time I'd have to eat cereal with tepid milk.

Farmor had gone to her room. It was the time of day when she always opened the windows and put the bedclothes out to air.

I hurried into the kitchen and put my letter in the Kremlin.

Farmor,

Don't worry if I'm late back from German. We'll phone you. Love to the Demetrias, if they come this evening.

Bye Farmor,

Tina

Every day when I left for school. Farmor went to the door with me, and waited there until I'd turned the corner. She never kissed me goodbye, nor I her.

Today, on reaching the corner, I turned and looked at her, and raised my little finger, as they do in Aachen when they say hello and goodbye.

Eight thirty, the time we start school, like he said. I hadn't been to St George's Square very often, but I remembered the way and found it easily enough.

I sat on a bench and watched the three half-naked bronze children hugging the lamp in the middle of the square. Nine o'clock, and he still hasn't appeared. Perhaps he's washed his hair and he's waiting for it to dry? The plane leaves at ten to twelve, so we have time.

I got up and began to look at the shops around the square, and to read the signs, telling myself that as soon as as I finished doing that, I'd see Wick suddenly appear, with his hair looking bright, like honey.

Café Skafidas. Panorama. Bakery. Dionysos. Doors, Windows, Security Locks. Mini Market. Butcher. Pizzeria Bella Italia.

Wick nowhere in sight. I look all round the square again:

Café Skafidas. Panorama. Bakery. Dionysos. Doors, Windows, Security Locks. Mini Market. Butcher's. Pizzeria Bella Italia.

No sign of him. Once more from the beginning:

Café Skafidas . . .

When I got to *Dionysos*, a restaurant, I saw a clock in the middle of the wall; maybe it was fast. A quarter to ten. I carried on:

Doors, Windows, Security Locks. Mini Market. Butcher. Pizzeria Bella Italia.

From the start all over again, and a quick walk as far as *Dionysos*. Ten o'clock exactly. They say when there's traffic, you need an hour to reach the airport. Oh, let him come now, right now. Once more from the start:

Café Skafidas . . .

I walk up and down the square three times. Now the clock on *Dionysos* says eleven, so does my watch. I stop and sit on the bench. Then I go and stand underneath the lamp with the children's statues, so Wick will see me from whichever direction he comes. What should I do? Where can I look for him?

I don't even have his phone number, and he's never told me where he lives, not even his proper name. Wick! Lady Di, she's the only one who'd know. 'Swear you'll never go there on your own.' Now all the promises are off, Wick. The plane will be leaving soon. Why aren't you here? Why?

I couldn't hold back my tears. I went slowly round and round the square, and suddenly I began to run, and my legs took me to Lady Di's. I rang the bell, hoping he would open the door. It was her, Lady Di. She was wearing a shiny black jacket, as if she was about to leave the house. She'd put on eye-liner and dark lipstick. It was almost black. She looked round, as if searching for somebody.

– On your own? Where's Stavros?

So Wick's real name was Stavros!

– Isn't he here? I asked.

– No, I haven't seen him since yesterday evening.

I began to shake.

– What's wrong? Come in for a moment.

I went in and asked her for some water. I took a sip, but I couldn't swallow properly.

– I've been waiting for him the whole morning. We were supposed to meet, I stammered.

What should I do? I had to tell her about the planned journey because she had to find Wick for me, immediately. Maybe they'd change our tickets for tomorrow.

– Hurry up, tell me what you want, I'm just going out. You caught me at the front door.

I try to find the right words:

– We were going to leave. At a quarter to twelve. The plane to Frankfurt. Then the train – to Cologne and Aachen. We had money. I gave him a lot of stamps. He went to the stamp-dealer you introduced him to.

Lady Di looked at me for a few moments with a baffled expression, then she burst out laughing:

– So that's why he came here yesterday with a small fortune? And you, you little idiot, you thought you were going on a journey?'

– What? You're lying!

I took her by the shoulders and shook her. I was shouting, I must have been screaming. She tried to cover my mouth; I bit her hand. She pushed me away, and I fell over. I was shaking uncontrollably.

– Stop carrying on like that. I've got to go, I'm telling you.

I couldn't stand up. I couldn't stop the shaking. Lady Di was whirling around the room like a big black bird. For a moment, I lost it completely. Then she came back over to where I was lying. With a struggle, she managed to grab my arm and hold it down by standing on it with her foot. The rest of my body was thrashing around. She tied the rubber strap round my arm. I scarcely felt the prick of the needle; my veins can't have been very deep.

Gradually, I stopped shouting and kicking out. I felt a warmth spreading all over my body and a gentle calm. Everything dropped away. I didn't care any more about missing the plane. When I opened my eyes, I saw owls flying around the room. I jumped at the sound of the doorbell. As if in a dream, I heard the door open.

– What have you done? Wick's voice, angry.

– What have *you* done? You should have seen the way she was carrying on. I had no other way to calm her down and I absolutely have to leave. If I don't keep my appointment, my father will cut off my allowance. I couldn't leave her here on her own freaking out like that.

I heard two loud slaps on the face.

Why are Wick and Lady Di arguing? As for me, I'm feeling fine, as if I'm floating in the ocean. What did she say his name was? Stavros. Doesn't suit him at all. I'll tell him.

I try to speak, but no words come out of my mouth. Wick came up close. His hair was dirty.

– How are you feeling?

I try to say 'absolutely fine', but the words get mixed up. And Wick is going round and round me as if he's doing a dance.

– If anything happens to her, I'll make sure you take the rap.

Who's he talking to? Who'll take the rap? I felt his hands lifting me up. I can fly, Wick, you don't need to lift me, I can fly I'm not a blind cormorant, I said, but apparently only to myself: the words stayed inside me.

He went out onto the street holding me in his arms. Why's he running so fast? Of course, so we can catch the plane.

Then he stopped. He put me down. It's cold on the marble. He rang a doorbell loudly, then I heard his footsteps, as he ran off.

A door opened.

Farmor!

And I was flying, flying, except that somehow I was being held back because one of my wings was broken.

CHAPTER TWELVE

I'm struggling, fighting to free myself from the spider's web. With one arm. Someone's holding the other one. It's difficult, because some of the owls have also got tangled up in the netting. They're trying to help me, pecking away at the thousands of threads in the web, opening it up like a curtain. Then they fly away.

I rest my arm on the bedclothes. A feather duvet. I've arrived in Aachen.

I open my eyes. A man I don't know is holding my hand and smiling at me. He turns his head and speaks to someone else:

– She's come round.

I look all around me. I'm not in Sigrid's house. But the bed is a large one. I'm sitting up on the pillows. Opposite me are the three Demis, and Farmor in her coffee-coloured armchair. What am I doing in Farmor's room?

– A good job you called me in time, Eleni, says the stranger.

– Not to mention the luck I had, finding you straight away, replies Eleni, who has the voice of

Little Demi. She's almost whispering, but I can still hear her.

– How are you? the unknown man asks, and carries on holding my hand, as if feeling my pulse.

I don't reply. I just give a brief nod.

– But didn't you notice anything, Ismeni?

Little Demi's voice, just about reaching my ears.

– No, Demetria, not a thing, says Farmor, sounding as if she has a throat infection.

'But didn't you notice anything, Tina?'

'No, Farmor, not a thing.'

The stranger takes hold of my hand again, but not to feel its pulse. He lifts the pyjama sleeve and looks under it very carefully. Then the other hand.

– As I said yesterday, Ismeni, there's only one needle prick.

I felt something prick my heart. Yesterday? And now it's today?

– I'll go and make some coffee, says Little Demi.

– No! I shout, as everything comes back to my mind: the coffee jar and the journey and Lady Di with the black lips and the rubber strap and Wick, who picked me up in his arms and ran . . .

Little Demi is smiling:

– The coffee's not for you, I'm just making it for us and for the doctor, we've been up all night.

All night? That means it's certainly the day after. Now she'll go to the Kremlin tin . . . I guess Farmor hasn't drunk any coffee from the time she found me on the marble doorstep. So now Little Demi will find the letter. I begin to shake. The stranger – I realise he's Little Demi's nephew, the doctor who went along with them to the Kurds – holds my hand.

– Calm down . . . Everything will be all right . . . As long as it doesn't happen again. Once you've recovered, you can tell us all about it . . .

Then he turned to Farmor:

– No, don't get up, Ismeni. I don't need another patient.

– Yes, Ismeni, he's right, we were really worried about you too, yesterday, said Smart Demi.

– But why didn't I notice anything? said Farmor, in a hoarse voice.

Big Demi was wiping away a tear that was running down her cheek. Anyone would think I'd died. Then I remembered, the coffee is coming, and I don't have any pills to give me a lift . . . I don't have anything or anyone. Not even Wick . . .

I caught the smell of coffee. Little Demi came into the room with a tray – my heart was almost at bursting point. She put the tray on a side table, came up close to me, and stroked my forehead.

– You're a brave little soldier – there's nothing to be afraid of.

I remember hearing that Little Demi had been tortured back in the days of the Occupation – she was only sixteen – to try to get her to betray her comrades. 'They never got a word out of her, although they nearly finished her off,' said Smart Demi. Little Demi used to laugh: 'Big deal, there were plenty of others they shot.'

She left me and was quietly handing out the

coffees. She didn't betray me either. Wick had let me down, and everything was ruined. But he had picked me up in his arms and taken me home. So that was why he didn't want me to go on my own to Lady Di. Because of the needle. Did he care about me? He'd given her those two slaps on the face. Wasn't her fault . . . She didn't know what to do when I started freaking out . . . Really, it was his fault . . . Yes, yes, it was his fault. Everything was ruined. We were done for . . . I began to drift off again.

I opened my eyes. He was standing over me, with his curly hair and his deep blue eyes. Only thing missing was a pair of wings. Vasilis. I tried to smile, but couldn't manage it. Next to him a girl wearing a bright green pullover – I'd never seen a sweater look so green.

– Tina, Marina has come to see you as well.

– Thank you, whispered the good little girl, lying on the big bed covered with the feather duvet. A massive duvet, for only twenty coupons. Gran hadn't yet managed to take it to the poor Kurds.

I closed my eyes again, so as not to see the chest of drawers opposite the bed, so as not to imagine the top drawer opening of its own accord and the stamp album falling out and showing its empty pages.

I could feel Farmor was there, because she'd grabbed hold of the foot of the wooden bed so tightly that it made me shake. Where was she sleeping, then? In my narrow little bed? I heard her voice:

– Mr Benos, I rescued my husband from the clutches of the Germans, do you really think I won't be able to rescue this girl from the clutches of these people . . . She just has to tell us . . .

Silence. Then I hear Vasilis speaking:

– I'm afraid, Ismeni, that these clutches can be even more cruel than those of the Nazis.

I opened my eyes. Farmor was standing straight in front of me, with her eyes shining like they were in the photo of her carrying the rifle.

So who's going to tell you, Farmor? Tina? She's not going to breathe a word, not about Wick, not about Lady Di. Even if they torture her like Little Demi.

– Would you like some milk? asked sweet little fairy tale Granny Farmor.

– Yes, but cold, from the fridge, replied Konstantina with the determined look.

– Fine, I'll bring you some.

I stayed alone with Vasilis and Marina. Their hands holding mine were warm, even warmer than the feather duvet.

Farmor and I are putting on an act, so that no one will say we've been lying to mum and dad.

– Konstantina has bronchitis again.

It's not really a lie. I don't know how I caught bronchitis while I was snuggled under my duvet. The doctor says my 'condition' may have something to do with it. My 'condition' . . . ?

Every time Farmor gives me a dose of syrup, she

takes the bottle away with her. *'But didn't you notice anything, Ismeni?' 'No, Demetria, nothing. I didn't even know that German cough syrup can be . . . '*

I asked if I could go back to my room. Farmor says first of all my fever has to go down before I can get up. And in my room there isn't space for a chair for anyone to sit down. I don't care if they stay standing. I can't bear being in Farmor's room any more, with the chest of drawers directly in front of me and the four women hassling me – even if they do it very sweetly:

– Tell us.

– Tell us.

– Tell us.

– Please, just tell us.

I'm speechless, like I was when I was an infant. 'You should take her to see the doctor. That child won't speak, not even a peep out of her.' When I pretend to be asleep, I can hear them talking among themselves.

– Where did she get them?

– She just goes to school and comes home again.

– And then from home to her German class.

– I've heard that they wait for the kids outside the schools, so they can sell them . . . , said Big Demi, but she was interrupted by Farmor's angry voice.

– How can you sit there and tell me that? Do you think Konstantina could be accosted by a stranger and he could sell her drugs as if they were chewing gum? Something else has happened here, something I can't even imagine.

– But didn't you notice anything, Ismeni?

– No, Demetria, not a thing.

– Well, I said that I thought there was something wrong with the child.

– She has to tell us where she got them.

– Yes, she'll have to tell us.

– She'll have to.

Vasilis, Mr Benos, comes every evening, sometimes on his own, sometimes with Marina. They're all waiting for him to ask me questions. But he doesn't.

I'm back in my little room. The duvet is too big for the bed, and Farmor has tucked it in at the sides and at the bottom. I creep underneath it to bury myself inside.

Herr Heiner was pleased to see me, and came up so I could stroke his head through the bars of the cage. Little Demi has taken on the task of feeding him and cleaning his cage.

Farmor gives me another dose of cough mixture and takes the bottle away with her. Oh, I wish I could finish the lot, so as not to have to think any more.

The bell rings. The Demis are inside, drinking their coffee. Vasilis and Marina never come this early. I'm snuggling down inside the duvet and pretending to be asleep. But I throw off the bedclothes straight away when I hear Marina's voice. I can't hear anyone else. Strange, she's come on her own. I expect her to appear in my room, so I open my eyes. But she doesn't come. She's talking with Farmor and the Demis.

– I came for a chat about Tina.

– She's asleep.

– All the better.

I sit up in bed and try so hard to stretch out my ears to listen, I imagine them growing like those of Pinocchio's friend who became a donkey. Wick should be a donkey too, like his namesake. Then at least he'd have an excuse for what he did to me.

Marina has a gentle voice, but she speaks clearly, so you can't miss a word.

She says she's talked things over with Vasilis, and they've agreed that she should come and have a chat with them. When she was nineteen, she had a really bad experience too.

– Drugs? asked Big Demi.

– Heroin, first time.

– What, you?!

I heard someone give a sob – it sounded like Farmor.

Marina had been, as she told it, a happy girl, without any troubles. She was doing a diploma at the School of Fine Arts in Athens. She got on extremely well with her parents . . . They were both architects, both worked very hard. They left home in the morning and came back late in the evening. At a party, she got to know Niko, who'd just returned from Paris where he'd been studying . . . He made a big impression on her, he didn't seem at all Greek. He looked rather like the Russian poet Mayakovsky.

– Mayakovsky!
– Mayakovsky!
– Mayakovsky!
– Mayakovsky!
Four voices full of admiration.

I didn't know who this Mayakovsky guy was, but they sounded as impressed as if Brad Pitt had walked into the room.

Marina carried on talking.

The whole evening she couldn't take her eyes off him. He spoke so beautifully, about Paris, about art. Suddenly, without her being aware of it happening, he was sitting next to her. He told her he was bored with the party, and if she liked, they could leave together. She was utterly fascinated by him, and they went out onto the street.

– That evening the great adventure of my life began. I was afraid I might lose him, but also curious to discover the universe he'd promised me . . .

I was tired of straining to hear. I couldn't catch every word, and I really wanted to know everything about Marina's great adventure, even if I was cross with her for seeing someone else – who could possibly be more wonderful than Vasilis? I got up and sat on the other side of the bed, to be closer to the open door.

Only Marina's voice could be heard, not a word out of Farmor and the three Demis. Just like back in Mikro Horio, when Captain Trap was telling his stories.

– I gave up everything. My studies, my home,

my painting, my friends. We lived together in a large house with antique furniture. It was his grandmother's, who'd died shortly before. We didn't go anywhere, we didn't see anyone. We could hardly be bothered to eat – or even wash. We just held hands and thought we were two exceptional beings, and nothing earthly or mundane could touch us. We lay down on his grandmother's bed, injected each other, and Niko would say that he could see the whole universe, whilst all I saw was a cloudy sky. Still, I was in his arms, and that was enough for me. When there wasn't a grain of powder left, he'd go out with his eyes on fire, and hunt around for it for hours. He always had money. Secretly his mother gave him as much as he needed. He'd assured her he was in therapy.

– I'd told my parents I wanted to live with him. They had no objection. I was old enough to make up my own mind . . . They asked to meet him. I said, later on. They went to Japan for a while on a work project. When they came back, I'd go home every so often, on my own. I made sure I was clean, smartly dressed, and above all that I wasn't showing any needle marks . . . They said I'd got thin, but they didn't have time to concern themselves with me. They were up to their eyes in work. Later on, of course, once they'd realised, they dropped everything to help me.

– I lived like that for three months. Niko couldn't exist for a single day without . . . seeing the universe. I begged him to stop, even just for a bit. He told me if

I wanted to, I could leave. He couldn't stop. I didn't leave.

– One day when I went to see my parents, I was there for hours, because they'd been late getting back from work. They asked me to stay the night, so they could see me for a bit longer. I decided to stay. I phoned Niko several times – but he didn't pick up. I assumed he'd gone out to see his dealer, to get more drugs.

– I slept really well back in my old bed. Niko didn't answer the phone. I left my parents' house in a state of panic.

– I unlocked the door and went straight to the bedroom. The bed was empty. I found him lying in the bathroom, not moving at all.

– Did he recover? asked Big Demi.

– Why are you asking her that? Don't you understand? said Smart Demi.

– I didn't know you could just go and . . . said Farmor in an agitated voice, without finishing what she was saying.

– The terrible thing, Ismeni darling, is that we didn't know anything about it, murmured Little Demi.

I'd got tired, and my eyes were closing. I crawled back to my usual place in the bed.

Soon Marina came into the room. So beautiful, so neat and clean, with wine-coloured velvet trousers and a white pullover. How could she neglect herself just to please this . . . Mayakovsky?

She bent down and kissed me. Since the time I left Aachen, no one had hugged me or kissed me. Every evening mum and dad used to put me to bed. 'Goodnight, Tina.' 'Sweet dreams.'

Sigrid used to kiss me too, and so did her mum, and even her grandmother, when she came to visit. Even Frau Sabrina used to kiss me. But here, nobody ever has, not one single time.

I reached out and hugged Marina and kissed her back. I decided to forgive her for seeing someone else before Vasilis.

– Get some rest so you can get better, and then Vasilis will come and we'll all have a talk.

She kissed me again and stroked my forehead.

– Settle down, my darling.

I snuggled down with the duvet up to my neck. 'My darling'! I didn't even need the cough syrup. 'My darling' . . . I fell into a sweet, gentle sleep.

By the time I woke up, it was evening. The door was open, and there was light coming from the sitting room, and I could hear them talking, but only in a murmur. I recognised Vasilis's voice.

I got out of bed, put on a cardigan and socks, and went to join them.

– Well, hello Tina! said Vasilis, and got up to put his arms round my shoulders.

Farmor, the Demis – except for Big Demi – and Marina, were all sitting round the table, which was piled with papers, brochures, books. They were reading with such concentration, you'd think they were going to have exams the next day. Marina wasn't reading. She was turning the pages of a book.

– Big Demi is making you chicken soup, said Farmor, without raising her eyes from what she was reading.

– You'll see, she's a wonderful woman, said Marina. She's saved so many lives, so many souls. When you read her book, you'll understand. My parents first turned to her to find out what they had to do, and it took another two months before I decided to go along myself.

– Did they have to see her several times? asked Farmor.

– Oh yes, a lot. With other parents who had kids with the same problem. But she's not the only one. Have a good look through the brochures. There are all kinds of places where you can find people with determination, experience, and love, who can give you support even when you're feeling down. You just have to reach out your hand. As long as you have the will to do so.

I bent over the table. There were heaps of strange words written on the covers of the brochures. TRANSITION . . . INTERVENTION . . . ARIADNE PROGRAM . . . NAVIGATION . . . EIGHTEEN PLUS . . . Sounded like the names of boats to me. What was the name of that ferry boat we'd taken to Aegina?

Farmor and the three Demis scanned one brochure after another. It reminded me of Vicky, just before we go in to an exam, the way she flicks through the pages of her books, hoping she might pick something up at the last moment.

Only Big Demi wasn't reading. She got up and brought me an egg-and-lemon chicken broth. It smelt wonderful. She put the plate down on a table next to me. I began to eat very slowly. It was really delicious.

– The rate you're progressing, I can see you going back to school in a few days, smiled Mr Benos.

I didn't reply.

– You don't want to?

– Course I do, I said finally, since he'd had to ask three times, but I was dreading the thought of going back there.

I'd finished my soup when I saw Farmor look up from what she was reading, and say in a really kind voice that didn't sound at all like her:

– And when Tina has made a decision, we'll go together to see this lady you were telling us about, Marina, or one of the others . . .

– Tina isn't going anywhere, I butted in.

It was like the time I came back from Proussos, when I'd swallowed my first blue pill and I wasn't afraid of anything or anyone.

– I'm not going anywhere, and I don't want any more questions.

Who knows what had got into me. They all lost it completely, even Vasilis. I was shaking from head to toe, and I glared at them with my determined look.

It was Smart Demi who broke the silence.

– Well, Ismeni, it's better not to say anything before we've done our homework.

They all laughed. Even I was smiling. Marina came up to me and gave me a hug.

– Tina, it's up to you, whatever you decide, and when you really want to know . . .

– I already know, I said stubbornly, and turned to go back to my room without looking at any of them, not even Vasilis.

Before I buried myself under my duvet, I heard Farmor's voice:

– You're right, Mr Benos. It's all much more difficult now than it was under the Germans.

CHAPTER THIRTEEN

Everything seems quite strange. I'm still not going to school because I'm very weak. Dad phones every evening. Mum is well, but she's still in bed, waiting for Mr Michalis's child to be born. Dad has sent us three more bottles of cough syrup with someone who was coming here from Aachen. There's not much I can do with them. Farmor keeps them under lock and key. And Sigrid keeps phoning and asking me in a whisper, when am I coming to stroke the horses at the station? 'Never', I reply, in a fit of exasperation. It's not her fault, poor thing. I'll write to her. But what can I say?

Farmor and two of the Demis go out 'to study' every evening. They go to the place Marina suggested. To learn about all kinds of stuff that they'd never in their lives imagined they might have to know about. Big Demi stays with me and prepares the evening meal.

The whole morning I'm with Farmor, just the two of us. She comes into my room every so often and asks me if I want anything. I'm dying to say: 'Just leave me alone!' but I can't see any reason to pick a quarrel. The old Farmor I knew has vanished. We don't come to blows over every word. Now she just paces up and down, makes a fuss of me, brings me my meals in bed, but it's as if she's waiting for something. I know what it is – she's waiting for me to say I want to go with her to that place, and tell them about everything that's happened. She'll be waiting a long time. She gets really impatient, asking me all the time:

– Well, Konstantina?

– Well, Farmor? I say, at least doing her the favour of replying the first time, though that's all I say.

Then she shuts up, picks up her brochures and goes to her room to find out how to treat someone who takes 'substances', as they called them at our school in Aachen.

Farmor isn't a good student. She seems to be struggling with her lessons. I'd never heard her sigh before but now, sometimes when she's reading, I catch her groaning: 'Uuuuuh!'

Big Demi and Little Demi also do a lot of pacing around, and I see them looking a lot more thoughtful than they used to. I imagine they're longing for the time when the Germans were around, so they could scramble into lorries, shoot Nazis, rescue grandad and disappear into the mountains. But what should they do with this girl called Tina who's never going to tell them about Wick, about Lady Di, not even about the little owl! And if I am in a hurry to get back to school, it's only because of Wick, and the chance of finding him waiting for me on some street corner.

If he brings me a pill, I'll forgive him. But it seems to me they've decided not to let me go back to school too soon. They're afraid someone will come up to me and sell me something dangerous. What they don't realise is that it's me who'll be running up to Wick.

And then what? The same again! First way up high into the sky, then way back down to earth with a crash. And more lying to Mr Benos, to Marina, to all of them!

Last night, I dreamt I was in Aachen. I'd gone to the ice stadium with dad. He was waiting for me, as usual, outside the skating rink. He was wearing a fur hat. The rink was empty. It was just me gliding around on my skates, with one leg in the air. I went up to the metal railing around the rink, and stopped next to dad. 'Look at how well you can skate! Next time I'll have to bring mum to watch you.' 'Where did you find that hat, dad?' 'It's Russian.' 'I'll tell Farmor, she'll like that.'

I gathered speed and went off skating around the rink again. Suddenly, from the opposite side, a couple came towards me. I recognised the girl immediately, it was Marina but the man holding her hand wasn't Vasilis, but the other man, the tall one who looked like Mayakovsky. He did a spin, lifted Marina up high with one arm, then they were slithering around as if they were going to fall over on the ice. And she was laughing and laughing. I tried to go up to them to ask about Vasilis, but they disappeared, as if the ice had swallowed them up.

Then I saw a skinny figure approaching from some way off, trundling around on the ice. He came up to me. His hair was blowing in the wind and it smelt like honey. But he wasn't wearing skates! He slid around barefoot on the ice with a rubber strap tied round one leg. He did a few jumps, and threw confetti into the air. The bits of coloured paper drifted down. I went to catch one. It was a stamp. The floor of the skating rink was strewn with stamps. 'Wick', I called. But he'd vanished. Dad had vanished too. The rink was empty, and I couldn't carry on gliding around because the ice was melting, melting. I tried to catch hold of the bar, but when I gripped it, it was as soft as dough . . .

I opened my eyes. It was pitch-dark, and I was gripping my duvet with both hands. I switched on the bedside lamp. Three in the morning. I felt thirsty.

I got up to go to the kitchen. I went into the hallway. There was a chink of light beneath Farmor's door. I stopped short and listened for her footsteps. She's never been able to sleep. I can hear her opening and closing drawers, looking for something. The stamps? If she sees they're missing, there'll be hell to pay. Unless they've advised her not to tell me off, at that place she's going to, and she's taken their advice. I'm guessing the doctor must have prescribed her some pills, and however well she's hidden them, I might be able to find some. But I scarcely make it to the kitchen before she's there beside me. She sees I've opened the door of the fridge.

– Are you hungry?

– No, I was thirsty.

She pushes me gently aside and closes the fridge. She gets a glass and fills it with water from the bottle on the table. I take it, turn my back and go to my room.

Oh, Wick! Right now I'd have been in Aachen, drinking cold milk from the fridge.

I lay down on my bed but I couldn't get back to sleep. I wondered if Wick was worrying about what happened to me after he left me on the cold marble doorstep . . . Unless he'd been to the school to ask Vicky where I was. Because Vicky had been sending me notes and wishing me 'get-well-soon' via Mr Benos. But then, why would Wick want to let Vicky know that he was interested in me? And even if he did ask her, I'm sure she'd just say she doesn't know.

On the other hand, perhaps he's been reading the death notices in the papers to see if I'd died . . . And with those thoughts, I fell asleep.

Morning. I look at the alarm clock on my bedside table. Eleven o'clock. I've slept late . . . Farmor's footsteps come and go in the house. The doorbell rings. Might be the doctor – he said he'd drop by to see how I am. I can hear Farmor opening the front door and talking to somebody.

– If she's not asleep, come in and see her.

– Farmor standing at my bedroom door .

– A girl has come from your German class to see how you are. Nora, her name is. As you're awake, I'll tell her she can come in.

Nora? I don't know any Nora. And anyway, I haven't made any friends in the German class.

She came into the room, a girl with scraped-back hair and a ribbon round her forehead. She was wearing a dark-coloured skirt and a little check jacket. Deep blue eyes, no make up. So Lady Di's name is Nora!

– I'll bring you an orange juice, Farmor says, coming in behind her.

We're there on our own, looking at one another.

– Are you OK? I wasn't really worried you know. I was really careful . . .

Farmor brought the orange juice.

– When you've finished your drink, just pop your glass on the table next to the hamster. There's space for it . . .

She stopped speaking and turned to leave. She closed the door behind her. That's one good thing about Farmor: she doesn't try to listen in.

Lady Di came up to me, I shrank back, and she sat on the edge of the bed. She took my hand and put something into my palm. It was the leather necklace and the wolf with the hole in his middle. My hand was trembling . . . There was a little piece of paper wedged into the hole. I nudged it with my finger, I pulled it out. It was crumpled in a tangle, like a tiny ball of wool. I unfolded it. Just one word written on it: 'Verzeihung'. The German word for 'Sorry'.

Lady Di, I mean Nora – somehow the name suits her – lowers her voice:

– He made me swear to bring it to you if . . .

She didn't finish, and before I could ask her any more, she began on another track:

– Your family, the doctor who treated you, didn't they ask you where you got . . . ?

– They did ask me – they ask me every day.

– Have you told them?

– No.

– You're not going to grass?

– No.

– Sure?

– Is that why you came? I asked, angrily.

– No, no, I promise. When I tell you, you'll understand. I just want to ask one more thing. Has your family contacted the police?

– No way. My gran hates the police.

– That's good, she said, obviously relieved.

I felt there was something she wanted to tell me, but she couldn't make up her mind. How pretty she looked like that, with no make-up and in those clothes. She looked like a little girl. I was wondering whether Wick might be sending me a pill, as well as an apology. I hung the wolf round my neck, tucked it under my pyjama top, and asked her:

– So has he sent me . . . anything else?

She gave me a scared look. Then she came closer, took my hand and whispered:

– He told me to bring you the wolf, if he left.

– He's gone! I barely held back a cry.

Even after I'd forgiven him . . . this was too much to bear. He'd gone on his own!

– He's gone, for ever.

– To Germany?

– No, they found him on a boat going to Aegina. With a needle stuck in his leg. I told him to be careful about the dose, but he wouldn't listen. Some people from his neighbourhood told me. And then I read it in the newspaper. What the hell was he going to Aegina for? . . .

I couldn't understand, or rather, I was only just beginning to understand. I broke out in a sweat.

– Is he . . . is he dead? I managed to stammer out.

Lady Di nodded.

– I have to go.

– Tell me everything.

– What else can I tell you? Don't shout like that – your grandmother will hear.

Inside I was shrieking, howling with rage, misery, despair. She got up and went to the door.

– Are you coming back?

– No, it's too dangerous. And don't come to see me, not ever. Bye.

– Tell me, Nora, please . . .

– My name isn't Nora.

CHAPTER FOURTEEN

I heard the door close. I buried myself under the duvet so Farmor wouldn't hear me crying. I held onto the wolf inside my pyjamas. He'd gone to Aegina to see the owl. *'I should stay here, with the birds. Maybe they could rescue me, too.'* But he couldn't even fly that far, just like the blind cormorant.

Oh, if only he'd washed his hair and we'd gone away together, to Germany. Now he'd be playing the piano, and his hair would be swaying to the rhythm of his fingers. I bit into the duvet, to stifle the sound of my crying. And then, everything misted over . . .

There I am, caught up in the spider's webs again. Now they're so dense, so tight, like a ball of wool, that I can't pull myself through them. Tina, the little owl, is there too, getting all tangled up in the webbing. Somebody's hand is untangling them. It looks like Mr Benos's hand – but then it vanishes. Once again the webs wrap themselves all around me. But there's the little wolf, without a soul. He's standing on his back legs, biting through the webs with his teeth. Where is he now, has he vanished too? No, he's come to sit on my heart, with the leather necklace dangling down onto the floor.

– Well you have got yourself in a tangle while you were asleep! My dear child, you're drenched in sweat.

Farmor's standing over me. She's holding the edge of my duvet in her hands. She's still beautiful, with no wrinkles, no age spots, just like she was when she was holding the rifle.

– Farmor, you know something, in your chest of drawers . . .

– You haven't woken up properly, you're still dreaming. I'm going to fetch a towel and some eau-de-cologne to freshen you up.

I tug at the hem of her dress.

– Farmor . . . tomorrow . . . I'm trying to find the words.

– Tomorrow – I'll go with you.

– Where?

– Where Marina said.

She didn't dare believe her ears.

– Are you sure you're really awake?

– Yes Farmor. Really.

She hugged me, then I felt her tears warm on my cheek. The Demetrias said they'd never ever seen her cry. Not even after she'd rescued grandad from the clutches of the Nazis. 'But these clutches, Ismeni, they're much sharper and more cruel than the Nazis.'

Next morning, Farmor called a taxi. The whole way there, she was holding my hand. I was wearing the orange pullover that Sigrid had given me as a present before I left Aachen. The little silver wolf was hanging from its leather necklace around my neck, and through its dark hole the orange shone like the sun. Neither of us said a word.

It didn't take us long to get there. A white house, freshly painted, with balconies full of flower-pots. We stood in front of the entrance.

Farmor turns and looks at me, smiling. She raises her little finger, just like in Aachen, when they greet each other. It's as if she wants to give me courage.

– Hi there, Tina.

I raise my own little finger.

– Hi there, Farmor.

Farmor presses the bell. The door opens, and we disappear inside.

Useful links

www.child.net/drugalc.htm

www.drinkanddrugs.net

www.drugfree.org

www.drugs-info.co.uk

www.drugscope.org.uk

www.erowid.org

www.fda.gov/oc/opacom/kids/html/7teens.htm

www.freevibe.com

www.streetdrugs.org

www.talktofrank.com

www.teenhealthcentre.com

www.teens.drugabuse.gov

www.teensurfer.com/drugalc.htm

www.theantidrug.com

www.usdoj.gov/dea/concern/concern.htm

Other books in this series

Blackmail **by Thomas Feibel**
A 17 year old goes in search of his rock idol but finds his life in danger when he mistakenly receives an email from gangsters...
ISBN 978-09551566-2-5 £7.99

Coming Back **by David Hill**
A story of recovery following a near fatal road accident involving a teen driver and a teenage girl.
ISBN 0-9542330-2-6 £7.99

Letters from Alain **by Enrique Perez Diaz**
An 11 year old boy comes to terms with the loss of his best friend after the family sets off in an open boat for America.
ISBN 978-09551566-4-9 £6.99

My Brother Johnny **by Francesco D'Adamo**
A young war hero tries to alert people to the reality of war.
ISBN 978-09551566-3-2 £6.99

Sobibor **by Jean Molla**
A 16 year old girl struggles with anorexia and disturbing family secrets.
ISBN 0-9546912-4-5 £6.99

Thistown **by Malcolm McKay**
A group of pre-teens try to make sense of rebellion and changing allegiance as the world around them falls apart.
ISBN 0-9546912-5-3 £7.99